# Niccolo

## By

# Eve Vaughn

## Dedication

I'd like to thank my readers for their continued support of my work. Writing has always been my passion and I appreciate the emails, shout outs and awesome reviews that mean the world to me. You guys give me the motivation to keep going.

And I'd especially like to dedicate this book to my father, because he asked me to. LOL. Love you Pop!

*She was the one he couldn't forget...*

Vampire, night club owner Niccolo Grimaldi has made a lot of hard choices. The hardest? Walking away from his child and the woman he could never forget. But for their safety, he knows he must stay away.

When witch, Sasha Romanova met Niccolo Grimaldi, she believed she had found the one who would love her, faults and all. That is until dark forces were used to keep them apart. When tragedy struck, Sasha and Niccolo sought comfort in each other's arms. But that one night of bliss doesn't last and Sasha is left to raise their son alone.

Years later, Sasha must come face to face with the man she never stopped loving when their son goes missing. In order to find their son before their enemies do, she must convince him to listen to his heart as they journey on a path of danger, intrigue and lust.

## Prologue

Moscow

The icy chill of the wind cut like a razor blade through anyone who dared to venture out. Those who didn't have the privilege of a thick coat wouldn't last long. Though he recognized the cold wisps of air swirling around him, it didn't affect him as adversely. Niccolo, however, hated winter, especially the ones in Moscow, because they were particularly more grueling than most other places. Though he was a vampire, he preferred warmer climates where he could bask in the warmth of the sun against his skin.

He breathed a sigh of relief once he arrived at his destination. The apartment building was not what he'd expected. It looked worn and run-down. Putting aside his surprise he stepped inside and immediately took note of the names over the mailbox and located number thirteen: a witch's number, of course. He climbed the stairs two at a time until he stood in front of the apartment he sought.

He banged impatiently on the door and tapped his foot in wait of a response. On the verge of knocking again, the door opened.

"Niccolo!" The small dark woman who answered the door looked up at him in apparent surprise.

He lifted a brow. "Aren't you going to invite me in?" Without waiting for a reply, he pushed past her into the tiny living quarters. "I'm not sure why you should look so surprised. Didn't you foresee my arrival?"

Sasha Romanova shook her head. "I don't have the gift of second sight. You know that."

Niccolo shrugged. "Do I? If you told me I must have forgotten."

Splotches of red colored her cheeks. "Perhaps because you didn't care to."

He could sense her hurt but in his mind, she had no right to play the victim after what she'd done. "I suppose you know why I'm here."

Fear registered in her eyes and her rosebud-shaped lips parted, but she said nothing.

"Yes, you should be frightened. Did you think you could keep him from me?" Niccolo was torn between shaking her senseless and taking her into his arms. *Dio!* He couldn't fathom how this woman could make him feel this raging lust, especially after her duplicitous act. Niccolo thought that after his sole slip-up with her, he would be sated, but one taste was apparently not enough. Nevertheless, he wouldn't allow a repeat of the events nearly three years ago on the night of Petra's crossing-over ceremony.

His cock twitched, and the heat generating from his eyes indicated that they were glowing. Niccolo mentally cursed himself for being aroused so easily by this deceitful little witch. Why her?

"Have you nothing to say for yourself?" he demanded when she didn't respond. The terror left her dark gaze to be replaced by something that looked remarkably like anger, an emotion she had no right to feel. He was the one who had been wronged.

She craned her head back to look him directly in the eyes. "How dare you burst into my home and make demands? At our last encounter, you couldn't wait to see the back of me. You've got a lot of nerve!" Her face had turned bright red in her fury.

"How dare *I?*" he asked, stunned by her audacity. "You kept my son a secret from me since his conception. And it's quite clear you performed some kind of spell to mask the connection I would obviously have felt when he was born. I had to be fucking told by my brother. You should have been the one to tell me! And you should be the one who feels ashamed." In that moment, he felt like wrapping his fingers around her neck and squeezing until she blacked out. No matter how badly he still wanted her, she done one of the most unforgivable things a woman could do to a man.

Sasha, however, didn't seem ready to be humbled. Instead she poked a finger in his chest and sneered. "Yes! How dare you! Whenever Petra was around, you acted as though I didn't exist even though there was a connection between us. Whenever we were close, the chemistry was so strong you could almost touch it. I know you felt it, because I did, too. You just couldn't get past the fact that I'm not as beautiful as my sister was. In fact, you are a shallow bastard, Niccolo Grimaldi."

"You know damn well that isn't true! And it has nothing to do with your hiding my son from me. Do you mean to tell me you did it out of spite? Was this your way to avenge yourself because you were just a convenient fuck for me?"

She gasped, taking a step backward as if he'd physically attacked her. Her bottom lip trembled, and his momentary triumph at seeing his barb hit its mark was short-lived. The wounded look in her eyes caused something within him to twist in pain and Niccolo couldn't figure out why. Finally, Sasha raised her head defiantly once again. "It has everything to do with it. Why are you so scared to face the truth? I loved you! Petra didn't give a damn about you. At least my love was genuine. You were just a trophy to her."

"Shut up!" he hissed through clenched teeth.

"I won't, because you need to hear this. There was a love spell cast on you. You didn't really love her."

"Shut your fucking mouth, liar!"

Sasha's dark eyes flashed. "I have no reason to lie. You were just another notch on her bedpost."

Niccolo was in front of her so quickly that she didn't have time to evade his grasp. His fingers shifted into talons that dug into her soft flesh. "You bitch!"

"Let go! You're hurting me." She smacked him hard.

The sharp sting on his cheek further incensed him. He shook her until her teeth rattled. Who was she to tell him how he felt? He had loved Petra. He had!

He still remembered how her silver-blonde hair had glistened in the sunlight, and the way her violet eyes sparkled when she was amused. How her tall, lush figure had given him many nights of pleasure.

He pushed Sasha away from him, more in disgust for himself than for her. "Where is my son?" he demanded.

Sasha hastily swiped at a tear that lingered at the corner of her eye. "After all this time you're still under the enchantment spell. You can't be trusted as long as the false memory of what you two supposedly shared haunts you. You might be older than me but I know far more about magic than you. And the one who enchanted you can keep you in her thrall for as long as the spell remains. That makes you dangerous. And I won't subject my son to that."

Niccolo wasn't interested in her lies. He'd come for one thing and one thing only. "Where is my son?" he demanded again. His fists were balled at his sides and he almost feared he'd lash out again, because if he did, he believed he might actually kill her.

A little voice spoke from behind them. "Mama, I'm thirsty."

Niccolo's steered his gaze to the small boy who stared back at him with obvious curiosity in his amber eyes. Eyes like his!

Sasha rushed over to the little boy, a miniature version of him. His hands shook and his heart pounded rapidly. An overwhelming feeling of joy and love filled his soul at the sight of this most precious child—created from his seed. He hadn't expected to be so overwhelmed with just one look.

After he had learned of his son's existence, he'd played this scenario in his mind a million times. But now that the moment was here, Niccolo was at a loss for what to do or say. The words remained lodged in his throat, threatening to choke him.

"Please go back to bed, and Mama will bring you a glass of water." Although she spoke to the little boy, Sasha looked at Niccolo with a pleading look in her eyes.

Niccolo slowly walked over to them and knelt down in front of his son. "What is your name, *piccolo?*" Niccolo asked softly. He reached out and grazed the boy's cheek with the back of his hand.

"Jagger," his son answered, giving him a big smile, which revealed perfect, tiny white teeth. Jagger stared at him so trustingly, almost as though he knew he was looking at his papa.

"Do you know who I am?"

Jagger shook his head.

When Sasha looked like she would say something, Niccolo glared at her. *Tread lightly, Sasha.* Her eyes widened as his thoughts projected into her mind, but she wisely didn't reply. He turned back to his son.

"I'm very pleased to meet you, Jagger."

The child reached out to touch his face, making Niccolo's heart melt. He knew in that moment that he would give his life for this child — his baby boy.

"I'm going to take Jagger to bed," Sasha spoke firmly as she stood up.

He wasn't happy about it, but he realized this wasn't the time to cause a scene in front of their two-year-old. His gaze never wavered from Jagger's small retreating figure until the boy was gone from the room.

Niccolo paced the floor, waiting for Sasha's return. An enchantment spell? No, that wasn't possible. He'd loved Petra, of that he was sure. It was apparent she'd only suggested such a foul thing because she was jealous of her sister. Sasha also did it to cover up her duplicity in hiding their son from him. There was no other logical explanation.

He didn't know how long he waited, but when she returned, he could detect the tracks of dried tears on her face. Good. She needed to cry and experience some of the pain he felt.

Niccolo studied her pale features. It was hard to believe she and Petra were sisters. Where Petra had been blonde and tall, Sasha was dark and petite, with shoulder-length sable hair and large, dark-brown eyes that looked almost black. She could never be classified as beautiful in the traditional sense of the word, but she was pretty with her deep red, bow-shaped lips, long, thick lashes, and a smooth, creamy complexion that seemed resistant to the sun's kiss.

He forced himself to tear his gaze away from those pretty red lips he had the sudden urge to crush beneath his. *Dio!* If anyone had put a spell on him, it was this witch. "Well?" he asked.

"Well, what?" A mutinous gleam entered her eyes.

"Why didn't you tell me about him? What is his full name?"

"Nikolai Jagger Romanov-Grimaldi."

"At least you acknowledge that he is my son."

"The Grimaldi is just a formality. It's not listed on his birth certificate."

A vein throbbed in his forehead as he fought to keep his ire beneath the surface. "From his middle name I assume you've continued your family's tradition for naming male children after their powers. What specific ability does he have and does he use it yet?"

"On a very small scale, but he does not realize what he's doing most of the time. His training won't begin until his thirteenth birthday. Like most of the males in my family he's able to manipulate metal. My brother Blade presented him with a platinum rattle. When Jagger touched it, the thing shattered into sharp jagged pieces. Jagger just popped in my head. No one expected him to display his abilities so soon. He'll be extremely powerful one day, possibly because he's a hybrid, and because of that I must keep him safe until he can fend for himself."

"Are you implying I can't protect my own son? You should have come to me the moment you knew you were carrying my child."

"Did you expect me to go looking for you after what happened? I thought what we had shared was special, but you discarded me like trash. I wasn't going to give you the opportunity to reject my child. I'd like you to leave my home now and never come back." She turned her back to him.

He stalked over to her and spun her around to face him. "You are insane if you think I will walk away from my son, just as you were foolish to think you could keep him a secret."

"I never kept him a secret. I ... I thought once you had finished grieving Petra you would come to me. I waited, but you never did. When Romeo spotted me with Jagger in Red Square last week, I knew he would tell you about what he'd

11

seen. I didn't deny it when Romeo asked if he was yours. How could I? Our son is the spitting image of you. It may have taken you a long time to find us, but you've come too late. Do the right thing and walk away."

"The right thing?" he asked incredulously. "The right thing is for a father and son to be together. Don't try to punish him and me for some imaginary hurt of yours."

"Imaginary? The hurt is very real, but even after all this time, you just don't get it. This isn't about me or you. It's about keeping Jagger safe." She went to the door. "Now, I'm very tired and would like to go to bed."

"I ask you again, what makes you think I'm willing to just walk away from my son?"

"If you really care, you will. I may not be much of a witch anymore, but I'm a good mother and I want what's best for Jagger. The night Petra died, we both knew of the threats made against you. Do you think I would allow my ... our son to become involved in your world?"

"All the more reason he should be with me. I can protect him and you."

"I've spent the last two years of his life protecting him."

"He's a vampire. He needs to be among his own."

"He's only half vampire. He is also a warlock. Deep down you know he'll be much safer with me. My brothers will be able to shield him from outsiders. Can you do the same? Can you guarantee that you would be there for him when you go on one of your missions, as you do so often? Will you be there when he's sick, or when he needs someone to hold his hand?"

"I can do that."

"Can you really? What kind of life will he have if he is constantly looking over his shoulder because someone wants to kill you?"

Niccolo wanted to argue with her and demand that his son come with him, but Sasha was right. Petra was dead because someone had tried to get him. He didn't know if he could bear it if the same fate befell his son.

Niccolo hung his head in defeat. He felt as though his heart were being ripped from his chest. Fate was cruel for making it possible to find his son, only to make it impossible for them to be together.

"Promise me one thing."

Sasha asked in a cautious tone, "What is it?"

"If he asks about me, I want you to tell him the truth. If he ever wants to find me, I want him to know that I'll be waiting."

Sasha nodded.

"Promise me! I want to hear you say the words."

"I promise." Her words were spoken softly but they seemed sincere enough.

"I'll make sure that the two of you are taken care of financially and should you ever need anything ..."

"I'll be in contact."

"When I find the rogues responsible for Petra's death, I will come back for him. Understand?"

"Yes," she whispered.

"I have to see him one more time."

She nodded. "Follow me." She led him down a narrow hall to a little room and opened the door. "I'll wait out here for you." Sasha stepped back to let him pass. Niccolo walked to the bed where his son slept peacefully.

A deep pain rushed through him; he felt like his world was caving in. Niccolo knelt beside the bed and stroked Jagger's small dark head. "My son, I'm so sorry I have to leave you when I've only just found you. There are so many things I want to tell you, make you understand, but you are still a *bambino*." A tear slid down his cheek. "It wasn't my intention to walk away from you like this, but your mama's right, it is not safe to be with me right now. But I promise you this -- when my enemies have been vanquished, I will find you, and nothing will keep us apart again. I swear this on my life. I love you, son."

# Chapter One

## Present Day

"Earth to Nico. Snap out of it!" Fingers snapped in his face.

Niccolo glanced at his brother. "Sorry, Ro. What were you saying?"

"I was saying there isn't a lot of action at the club."

Niccolo shrugged. "My clubs don't run like the rowdy bars you frequent. I'm sure you wish you were in the middle of one of your infamous rumbles right now. Don't you ever get tired of it?"

"Nope. You only have one life to live, unless you know a necromancer, that is. Why not live it doing what you love? And I love fighting and fucking. I've already done the latter tonight." The blond vampire grinned, his dark blue eyes twinkling with mischief.

A smile curved Niccolo's lips as he shook his head at Romeo's antics. It was times like these when he felt like the elder sibling instead of the other way around. He turned his attention back to the large glass wall in his office. From where he stood, he could see everything on the dance floor in the club below.

A small woman with dark hair caught his attention. Her back was turned to him so he couldn't see her face, but the sensual way she swayed her hips to the music made him wonder if she moved as fluidly in bed. When she twirled around, disappointment surged through him. He shook his head, in frustration for allowing his thought to stray to a woman who still haunted his dreams — the one he'd tried, but couldn't forget.

It was obvious he must still be firmly under the witch's spell. He'd been fighting it for years but had yet to shake these obsessive thoughts of her.

Romeo placed a hand of his shoulder. "Okay, spill it. What's on your mind?"

"What?"

"You haven't been listening to anything I've said all night. I could be hanging out with Wolf right now, busting some heads and getting my fill of pussy, not necessarily in that order. I'm not in L.A. often but I was hoping to spend time with you and do something fun besides watching you brood in the corner."

Niccolo sighed. "I'm glad you're here with me, Ro. I apologize for not being a more gracious host, but I suppose I do have quite a bit on my mind."

"Your trip to Russia?"

"Yes."

"You knew you would have to go back eventually, if anything to at least see Jagger."

"You know I can't make contact with him just yet."

"I realize that, but you'll eventually have to."

"I know, but we never did find those bastards who killed Petra. You know how my fondest wish is to be reunited with my son, but whenever we come close to finding answers, something else happens to fuck things up." Niccolo raked his fingers through his hair in frustration. "How do you think I feel to discover I've been wrong all these years? Someone wasn't only out to get me, but you, Marco, and Dante, too. I won't place Jagger in harm's way either. As long as his uncles and mother keep him cloaked from our enemies he's fairly safe."

It had torn him to pieces when he'd walked away from his child. A day didn't go by when he didn't think about Jagger, and wonder how things would have turned out if he had dared to take him all those years ago. It wasn't enough that he sent money to Sasha for Jagger's care, or that he paid someone to watch his son and take pictures when possible.

Whenever Niccolo returned home from a mission, he would take out his scrapbook of pictures and look at them before he went to bed at night. He had pictures from the time his son was a toddler to the present day. It was his only other connection to his boy. Well, Jagger was no longer a boy, but a man—a very handsome and well-rounded man as far as Niccolo could tell.

It was uncanny how closely Jagger resembled him. They shared the same jet-black hair, build, and amber eyes. The only things Jagger had inherited from his mother were her incredibly long lashes and full red lips. It didn't surprise him when his informant told Niccolo that Jagger was quite the lady's man. His chest swelled with pride at the thought of his son's prowess.

"While you were there, didn't you get a glimpse of him?"

"No. My trip was futile. As I suspected would be the case, the Romanovs weren't very forthcoming with any information. They still blame me for Petra's death."

"But you weren't even around when she was attacked."

"It doesn't matter. Those rogues had come for me. Had I been there, I could have protected her. Petra's family isn't particularly forgiving, especially her father."

"And Sasha? Did you see her?"

"No. She keeps away from her parents' compound and I didn't stay long in Moscow. I didn't think it was a good idea to see them as my visit would possibly draw unwanted attention."

"I hate to see you this way, Nico. Sometimes I think you've come to terms with the situation, but other times, I feel this deep pain radiating from you."

"How can I not feel pain? My son isn't in my life. He seems to be thriving without me. Keeping tabs on him isn't enough. Time hasn't made this an easy burden to carry either, in fact it makes the hurt grow rather than weakening it." Niccolo clenched and unclenched his fists. "He has suppressed his vampire side and is training to be quite the warlock under his Uncle Blade."

"Not under Ivan?"

"No. Apparently Sasha doesn't want her father to have anything to do with Jagger, and I'm inclined to agree with her. He's a cold, calculating man. He wasn't a particularly warm father toward Sasha, so there is no telling how he'd be around her offspring."

Romeo nodded in agreement. "I can't really say I blame her, either, but I wonder how she managed to wriggle from under his thumb."

"I don't know, but I'm glad she did. I can only imagine the hell he'd put Jagger through otherwise."

"You're a better man than I, because I would have taken my son with me."

"And have him suffer the life we have, the constant need to watch our backs because of who we are and yet without knowing why? Someone killed Petra because of me. And the attack on Maggie reaffirms that I've made the right decision."

"Well, you know how I feel about entanglements, but look at Marco. Despite the dangers of being with a Grimaldi,

Maggie has no problem being his bloodmate. They're both so disgustingly happy it almost makes you want to throw up." Romeo rolled his eyes.

Niccolo chuckled. "Do I sense a little jealousy?"

"Hell, no! I'm pleased our little brother has found happiness after everything he's been through. Maggie is a great woman who has proved herself worthy by standing up to that rogue. She and Marco are perfect for each other, but that kind of life isn't for me. I like coming and going as I please; a woman would try to curtail my activities—try to change me. After six hundred years, I'm too set in my ways. Besides, I just can't deal with all that lovey-dovey shit."

"I never realized you were this much of a cynic."

"I'm a realist. I have way too much fun living life on my own terms. I thought you did, too."

Niccolo narrowed his eyes. "What's that supposed to mean?"

"There was a time when you and I weren't so different. Wolf is like another brother to me, but he's not you. I miss when you and I used to raise hell together."

A small smile touched Niccolo's lips, but he felt no humor. "I guess you can say I finally grew up."

Romeo chuckled. "Are you implying I haven't?"

Niccolo shrugged. "I thought my meaning was pretty clear."

"Lucky for you I don't easily take offense."

"You know no insult was meant. Like you, I didn't think I would ever want to settle down, especially after what happened to Dante and Marco. The pain they suffered didn't seem worth it, but learning I'm a father changed that."

"Not when you met Petra? You were quite smitten with her."

"I suppose I was." Now that he looked back on it, that entire period seemed cloudy. He had been so sure he loved Petra that nothing else had mattered, but after her death, he could barely remember what he felt.

*You were under an enchantment spell.* Those words still haunted him.

Niccolo had been in Russia on a mission for the Underground when he first met Petra, a member of one of the most powerful warlock families in the immortal community. He didn't know how it happened, but he had fallen for her fast and hard. They had planned to marry, but everything suddenly came crashing down around them.

An anonymous source had left an urgent message for a meeting in St. Petersburg regarding the Romanov clan, but when Niccolo arrived at the designated location, his contact was nowhere to be found. It was only then that he had realized something was wrong. It had taken all of his vampire abilities to return to Moscow as quickly as he did, but still it had been too late.

By the time he entered the Romanov compound again, Petra was dead. All evidence pointed to rogue vampires, but there had also been the presence of one other: Sasha. Niccolo knew in his heart that she had not had anything to do with her sister's death, but in his grief, he had lashed out at her, as did her father.

Afterward, he had found it tough to sit through Petra's crossing-over ceremony, but it was later that night, as he was packing to leave the Romanov home, that he had betrayed her once again when Sasha had come to him.

He shook his head to dispel the memory.

"You know, Nico, I never thought I had any business saying this to you, especially since I try to mind my own affairs, but this thing you had for Petra ... It seemed so ..."

"Seemed what?"

"I can't quite put my finger on it, but when you talk about her, you get an odd gleam in your eyes. It's weird, because I can't feel you sometimes. In fact, I haven't been able to feel you for a while now. Your mind is cloudy and you've shut yourself off to me."

Niccolo lifted a brow in challenge. "Are you trying to say I've been bewitched? Because if you are, I'll give you that fight you were looking for."

"Hold on a second! You know damn well if I had something to say, I would come right out and say it. You never really talked much about that summer in Russia, but when you mention Petra's name, you get a sort of dazed look in your eyes. She was a witch. How do you know —"

"Romeo, if you care anything for me, you won't finish that thought. I loved her ... I must have."

"Sounds to me like the person you're trying to convince is yourself. Besides, it was Sasha who gave you a child. That's only supposed to happen with your bloodmate."

"Witchcraft."

"I never understood this animosity you felt toward Sasha. In fact, at one point I thought the two of you got along pretty well. It just doesn't make sense."

"I'd rather you didn't mention Sasha's name. I don't need this tonight. I'd appreciate you dropping the subject all together, *fratello mio.* I won't get on your case about your hell-raising and you can get off my back about Petra."

"Fine."

Niccolo felt like an asshole for hurting Romeo's feelings, but his feelings for his deceased lover remained a sore spot for him. Though he loved his brothers Dante and Marco, Romeo was the brother closest to his heart. No one understood him like Romeo and no one understood Romeo like he did. When their parents were killed, Dante had been so much older than they were and Marco was still an infant. He and Romeo had had to rely on each other.

Because there was only a two-year difference between them, they had been inseparable and would sneak off, give their elder brother a hard time, and cause trouble when they could. Niccolo usually followed Romeo's lead, never questioning his daring brother. It had been that way for over five hundred years, but his mission to Russia had changed everything.

Sometimes he wished he had turned down Dante when his brother had handed him the assignment. Then someone else would have gone in his place and Petra would still be alive. But if he hadn't gone, there would be no Jagger either.

Romeo broke into his thoughts. "I guess I should be moving on. I see I'm not really wanted around here."

Niccolo sighed. "Stop it. Of course you're always welcome here and I'm very pleased to see you. It's been over a month. I just have a lot on my mind so I'm sorry if I'm a bit short with you."

"Come out with Wolf and me tonight. It'll be fun. There's a little off-road bar not too far away. It's a little on the rowdy side — my kind of place. Hanging out with us might clear your head a little."

"No. I think I'll pass. I can't leave the club."

"You're the boss. Can't your employees handle things around here? I'm sure you wouldn't have hired them if you didn't think they were capable of taking care of this place in your absence. Come on. Live a little. I noticed the way you were eyeing that brunette on the dance floor." From his second-floor office, Romeo looked through the glass way to the crowd below and licked his lips. "How about inviting her up to your office and we can get a little pussy? The way she's moving, I bet she knows how to work those hips over a cock."

Niccolo zoned in on the dancing temptress. The brunette did look appetizing. She gyrated her bottom against her dance partner's crotch. As appealing as she was, he wasn't really in the mood. Tonight, he had the strangest sensation that something wasn't right.

"I'd only ruin the mood. I'm sorry."

"Well, if you don't feel up to it then I won't twist your arm. But you'd tell me if something was really the matter, wouldn't you?"

"Of course."

Romeo placed a hand on his shoulder. "Then tell me now. I may not be able to read you like I used to but I can still tell you're holding something back."

Niccolo realized Romeo had no intention of dropping the subject. "I can't shake the feeling that something is off. I don't know what it is though."

"Could it be Jagger?"

"I'm not sure. I spoke to my contact earlier who said that all was well, so I don't know what's bothering me."

"I know you want to keep him safe, but Jagger is a man now. Maybe it's time for you to meet him again. From what you've told me, he's been training under his Uncle so I'm guessing he should have a pretty good handle of his powers. He's no longer a boy, and you two will have to meet again eventually. Why not make it sooner rather than later. You know I'd back you up as would Dante and Marco."

"I'm sure you would, but Dante has the Underground to worry about and Marco has his new family to think of. This is my problem and I'll have to handle it on my own."

"But as long as this problem remains a distraction to you, are you really handling it? I'm going to head out now but I'll give you a call tomorrow. Perhaps we can hang out then.

Think about what I said." Romeo gave Niccolo's shoulder a light squeeze before removing his hand.

When his brother was gone, Niccolo took a seat behind his big metal desk and rested his head in the palm of his hands. Perhaps Romeo was right. It was time to see Jagger. But seeing his son also meant facing Sasha again and for reasons he couldn't explain, the thought of seeing her again made him nervous. And he didn't like it one bit.

<><><><><>

"Mama, it's time. I want to know everything about my father."

Sasha closed her eyes. She had dreaded this moment for nearly thirty years. It was inevitable this subject would come up. "Why have you finally decided to come to me about this? I thought ..."

"You thought that because I never mentioned it before, it wasn't something I would ever bring up?"

She bit her lip and nodded.

Jagger shook his head and sat down next to her, taking her hand in his. "Mama, we both know that was unrealistic. I'm twenty-nine years old, a year away from coming into my full powers as a warlock, but I feel as if a piece of me is missing."

Sasha leaned over to touch her son's face, so like his father's. He was tall, standing well over six feet, with wavy black hair, a beautifully sculpted face, and thickly lashed amber eyes. Jagger had been breaking hearts since the day he was born. She couldn't believe that someone so handsome had come from her womb.

"You could have come to me with any questions about your papa at any time. I would have answered them."

"*Da*. I know this, but it was difficult."

"Why?"

"I once overheard you and Uncle Steel talking about him. I'd never seen you look so sad before. Every now and then, you get that same look in your eyes and I know you're thinking about *him*. I figured it would hurt your feelings if I brought him up and I didn't want to do that. But I can't pretend any longer that his existence no longer matters to me. I'm different and there are things happening to me that I don't understand. But I'm sure my father would. I'm sorry if my bringing this up causes you pain, but I have to know."

She stroked his cheek to assure him she wasn't upset. "You shouldn't be sorry. You have every right to know about your father. In fact, I should have told you about him instead of you coming to me. I foolishly thought because you never mentioned him, you weren't interested. That was very short-sighted of me to think that. And I'm the one who owes you an apology."

"Mama, don't. You have nothing to apologize for. Just tell me about him."

She dropped her hand and bowed her head. There was a big gaping pain in her chest when she thought about Niccolo. She forced herself to control her emotions while she told her son what he deserved to know. "The most important thing you should know about him is that he loves you very much. I don't want you to ever doubt that. You are the most important person in his life."

Jagger's eyes narrowed. "Then why did he abandon us? Why did he never visit?"

"He wanted to be with you, he really did, but he couldn't."

"Why couldn't he?"

She blinked several times to keep herself for crying. She'd always known the time would come for them to have this talk. But no matter how many times she'd played this situation out in her mind it still didn't lessen the pain. "Just give me a moment, okay?"

"Mama, if it bothers you this much —"

She held up her hand to cut him off. "No. I'll be fine. You need to hear this."

Reliving all the old memories threatened to overwhelm her. She didn't know where to begin. Did she start at the part of her father's betrayal or Niccolo's?

Warlocks came into their full powers at the age of thirty, but witches did not come into their full powers until the age of one hundred. Despite this, witches could be more powerful than their male counterparts because their powers increased naturally with age. Warlocks, however, went on magical sojourns to increase their abilities and keep their powers at a level that would be difficult to challenge.

From an early age she had known she was a disappointment to her parents, especially her father. She'd been born small, dark, and plain, while everyone in her family was tall, blonde, and beautiful. Her skills as a witch did not live up to Romanov expectations; she hadn't been able to save Petra, and that she lived when Petra had died was the final and biggest disappointment.

Sasha was used to being negatively compared with her brothers and sister, but despite this, she and her brothers were close. She and Petra, however, never had much of a sisterly bond. When Petra had died her parents blamed her and called her the most hurtful of names. But when she'd informed them she carried Niccolo Grimaldi's child they'd all but disowned her. By then Niccolo too had let her down, which was when she realized the only person she could rely on was herself.

Her oldest brother, Blade, was in charge of Jagger's warlock training, but she had distanced herself from her parents, choosing to live outside of the Romanov compound to support herself and Jagger.

To her surprise, Niccolo sent regular payments to her through an agency for Jagger's upkeep. The payments were so generous that she didn't have to work if she didn't want to, but she made sure everything went toward her son. He received the finest clothes, went to the best schools, and she'd even been able to purchase a nice house. He provided enough for them to have a very comfortable lifestyle. She bartended on the side to occupy her time but all her earnings she saved. When Jagger was old enough to get a place of his own she forwarded all the money to him that Niccolo continued to send.

"Your father didn't abandon you. If he had his wish, he would have kept you with him."

"Then why didn't he?"

"He has some very powerful enemies. At the time, we felt it was for the best that he stay out of your life until the danger that surrounds him is gone."

"Obviously the danger must still exist since he hasn't seen fit to come see me." Jagger sounded bitter.

Sasha took his hands in hers. "He's been supporting you financially, hasn't he? Almost everything you have is because of his generosity."

Jagger practically snarled, "Money doesn't mean a damn thing. It doesn't replace him actually being here. You say he loves me yet I've seen no evidence of it. Financial support is all well and good, but what about the emotional support?"

Hearing the raw pain in son's voice tore her in half. She wished she could absorb his hurt so he wouldn't suffer. "All valid points. But like I said, he wanted to protect you. He did visit you once."

"I would have remembered that!"

"You were barely two. It was the first and the last time he saw you. He wanted you to come with him but I convinced him you would be better off with me. I'm the one you should be angry with. Not him. I wanted to protect you. I know it hurt him to leave you because the entire time he was here he was fighting tears. And when I tell you a man like him doesn't easily cry, believe it."

"If he really cared he would have stayed and protected me himself! Make me understand why it was so important for him to leave me. I thought vampires were protective of their kin and protective of them. Was I wrong? Is it because I am a half-breed that he doesn't come?"

Sasha was shocked. "No! You mustn't think that way! And half-breed sounds so negative. You're a hybrid. Be proud of that."

"How else am I supposed to think? I know nothing of my vampire heritage. I'm tired of being in the dark." Jagger stood up abruptly. "I want a name."

Sasha's swallowed, her stomach twisting in knots. There was no more stalling. "His name is Niccolo Luca Grimaldi. Your last name, before I shortened it, was Romanov-Grimaldi. That is why your first name is Nikolai, the Russian version of your Papa's name."

"Grimaldi? My papa is one of *the* Grimaldis?" His incredulous demeanor surprised her.

"You've heard of them?"

"Of course I have. Who hasn't among our kind? They are legends!"

"Yes, I suppose they have made a name for themselves in the immortal community." She smiled humorlessly.

"But why did he leave you alone? Why aren't you two together? I guess I'll have to believe you when you say he wanted to keep me safe, but what happened between you and him?"

She wrung her hands together nervously, wondering how much she should tell him. Upon looking at the bewilderment shadowing his handsome face she knew then he deserved the entire story. He was a man now and could handle it.

Jagger watched her with fervent intensity as she spoke, his steady amber gaze never leaving her face. She hesitated for a moment because he looked slightly feverish; even his eyes looked a little pink, but that wasn't possible because immortals didn't get sick. She banished the thought and continued her story.

"Since you've heard of the Grimaldis you probably already know what they do."

"Sort of."

"I met your father a little over thirty years ago. At the time I still lived with my family. Your father and his brother ... your Uncle Romeo ... came to our home on an information-gathering mission. They were on the trail of a rogue vampire their family had been chasing for centuries and thought my father would have some useful information for them. Papa invited them to stay. Romeo remained for a short while, but Niccolo, your father, chose to linger. I think I fell in love with him the second I laid eyes on him. In an instant I knew he was the man I wanted to spend all of eternity with, but ..." Sasha broke off. After all this time it still hurt her to think about how he'd spurned her, and talking about it was even more painful.

Jagger squeezed her hand, giving her some measure of comfort. His need to reassure her even when he was the one who probably needed it more swelled her heart that was already filled with love for him. He made her so proud. She didn't think she would have made it through the trying years without her him. "Take your time, Mama."

"You are a good son." She leaned over to kiss his cheek which felt warm. Sasha frowned. "Are you feeling well?"

"*Da*. Please continue."

She studied his face for a moment still noticing that strange pink tinge to his face. She made a mental note to question him about it later. "As I was saying, I fell hard for your father, but my sister wanted him, too. You've seen pictures of her. Your Aunt Petra was a great beauty, but unfortunately she knew it too. She was used to getting what she wanted, and she usually got it."

"And he wanted her, too?"

"In the beginning he didn't seem to. For a brief time, I thought he returned my feelings, but I soon found that he was no different from any of the other men who fell at my sister's feet. It tore me apart to see them together. When they announced they would be married, I think I died a little on the inside. In my heart he belonged to me, but I was so used to being in Petra's shadow and stepping aside so that she could shine, I didn't know what else to do." She sighed. "My parents, my father especially, supported the match. I suppose I could have pleaded my case with your father, but I didn't have the confidence or self-esteem to face him. My fear of getting my heart trampled on even more than it already had scared me more than you can imagine."

Sasha took a deep breath. Why did this have to be so difficult? "The Grimaldis have accumulated vicious enemies in their lifetime, and because of that, your aunt was killed."

"What happened?"

"One night, Niccolo received an urgent message from an unnamed source; I never did find out whom. My family was away visiting relatives. Niccolo, Petra, and I were the only ones in the compound when he received that missive. He told Petra he would return as soon as he could. He hadn't been gone for more than a few hours before four rogue vampires broke into our home. These rogues also practiced dark magic. Petra and I did not have enough power to fend them all off. One of the rogues knocked me out. When I woke up, Petra was dead. My parents and your father all blamed me for her death."

"But it wasn't you fault! And you were a young witch. How did could they expect your powers to withstand four rouges practicing the dark art?"

"Grief can be an irrational emotion. They knew I didn't kill her, but they felt there was more I could have and should have done. My father even wished that I had died instead of Petra."

Jagger's eyes widened in his apparent horror. "My father ... did he say this, too?"

"No. Your father was never deliberately cruel, but then again, he didn't have to say a word. His eyes said it all. Niccolo and Papa had a falling out shortly after Petra's death. During Petra's crossing-over ceremony, I went to Niccolo and one thing led to another—well, I don't need to tell you what happened next." She sighed again. "I thought we had shared something special, but when I revealed my feelings to him, he turned me away. A few weeks later, I discovered I was carrying you. I wrote to Niccolo, but perhaps my letter was lost. It wasn't until you were just about two years old that he discovered your existence. Since then he has taken care of you in the only way he could."

"Why did he never offer to do the right thing by you?"

"You mean marriage?"

"It would have been the honorable course of action."

"Even if he had, I'm not sure I would have accepted, at least not with things the way they were. There's no hope for me and your father."

"But you still love him, don't you?" he demanded.

"Yes," she whispered.

She was an idiot for still caring about a man who had never felt a thing for her except a brief moment of lust.

"Do you know where he is now?"

"He travels quite a bit and has homes all over the world, but I believe he spends most of his time in Los Angeles."

"I see. No, actually I don't. I don't understand how he can discard you so callously."

"Please don't get upset on my behalf. Regardless of how he feels about me, he loves you very much."

"How can I not get upset when I know how much pain you've suffered over him?" Jagger stood abruptly. "Look, I have to get out of here. I'll talk to you later." He leaned over to give her a brief hug.

She got up and followed him to the door. "Please, Jagger, don't leave like this. Where are you going?"

"I haven't decided yet." He kissed her cheek and left.

Sasha had a sinking feeling she knew exactly where he was going.

## Chapter Two

"You knew what the Council would say before you went there. They're a bunch of assholes. Why did you even bother?" GianMarco asked, raking his fingers though his shoulder-length blond locks.

Dante grinded his teeth in frustration and turned to look at his youngest brother. "It was still worth a shot. I'm grasping at straws here and any lead I can get would be helpful. I swear if I ever get Devlin Locke alone for two minutes, I will rip his entrails out and make him eat them," he vowed.

Marco nodded in obvious approval. "He's a sniveling waste of flesh. It seems pretty odd that a vampire who is not quite three hundred is head of the Council."

Dante felt the same way but knew Locke's appointment to the head of the Council was a political decision more than anything else. "He's heavily connected. The whole idea of the Council is nonsense anyway. That they would try to dictate how we should live our lives is a sham. Particularly when many of us have been around longer than the Council has been in existence."

"Is it possible the Council could be behind the attacks on us? I swear to God that if they are, I'll kill them all myself. When I think of what could have happened to Maggie—" GianMarco broke off.

Understanding how he felt, Dante patted his brother on the arm. The bond that Marco and his wife Maggie shared was so intense Dante was aware that the mere thought of losing his bloodmate caused Marco a great deal of pain. "If I thought they were responsible, I would gladly do it myself. I didn't get the impression they're behind the attack, but I have a sneaking suspicion they're hiding something."

The Council of Immortals had been a thorn in his side for as long as Dante could remember. Formed several hundred years ago by a warlock, vampire, and shifter, it began as a social organization for immortals. Over time, its purpose evolved. The Council decided immortals deserved their own communities, away from humans, so that they could be unashamed of their immortality. They also created a task force to police immortals who got out of line. In theory it was a good idea, but in practice, it was something different altogether.

Initially, Dante had had no problem with this arrangement, but as new and more outspoken members joined the Council, and it gained more support in the immortal communities, the council members grew pompous and annoying.

The Grimaldis and other like-minded immortals were seen as threats because they mingled with mortals and were considered renegades. That they weren't hunted down and killed owed to the fact that most of the Underground members were very powerful, and that no one except Dante and his brothers knew for sure how many agents there actually were. He had no doubt, however, that once the Council gained more support the order would be given to eliminate Dante, his agents, and his allies.

The Council shunned anyone connected with the Underground. Dante had vowed he would never ask them for anything, but when he realized the danger his brothers were in, he'd swallowed his pride. And what had he gotten in return? Locke had sneered at him.

*"Why should we help you, renegade?"*

34

*"Because the purpose of the Council is to prevent things like this from happening. How can you let Il Diavolo and his minions run wild?"*

*"Isn't that what your precious Underground is for, Grimaldi? Can't handle it, can you? And what a shame about your friend, Trent Black."*

The smug smirk of satisfaction on Locke's face was enough to make Dante pounce and tear the arrogant bastard's throat out but common sense held him at bay. The two shifters on either side of Locke had immediately changed to wolf form and growled at him, baring their large, sharp teeth. Two other vampires slowly stepped out of the shadows as Dante had held himself in check. Individually, he could have taken them all, but he knew they wouldn't fight fairly. Cowards!

It was unseemly how Locke was able to make these outrageous comments while the rest of the Council sat back and did nothing. But it was quite possible Locke had someone much more powerful backing his actions. It seemed the most logical explanation.

*Damn.*

He would give anything for two minutes alone with the head of the Council. Dante bet Locke wouldn't be so cocky then.

"If I find out that you know something about this, I will be back," Dante had threatened savagely.

"Aww, what's wrong, Grimaldi? Not so big and bad without your little brothers dogging your heels?" Locke had taunted.

Dante knew in that moment that one day he would kill Devlin Locke. After shooting a malevolent glare in the man's direction, he'd turned and left. He still couldn't shake the feeling they were keeping secrets, but it wouldn't have been wise at the time to take action without backup.

Marco spoke, bringing him back to the present. "The Council has never been a favorite of mine, either. What I want to know is who the hell Adonis is? We have no other relative I know of. You said Papa didn't have siblings."

"As far as I know he didn't. Whoever it is, he might be using that name deliberately, possibly to throw us off."

"Why do you think that?"

"It was Papa's middle name."

Marco frowned. He looked as though he were about to speak; instead, he turned toward the front door. A few moments later, Maggie walked into the living room, her arms laden with packages.

Marco's face lit up like a child's on Christmas Day. Dante could feel the intensity of his brother's feelings flowing from him.

"*Ciccina*, let me get those packages for you. Had I known you would be out this long, I would have gone with you." Marco took the boxes and bags from Maggie's arms.

"I was only gone for a couple of hours. Her smile was radiant giving her already pretty face an ethereal glow. Dante waited in tense anticipation for her to acknowledge his presence but she only had eyes for Marco.

"For such a short period, it seems you've managed to buy out the entire department store. I hope you had some help getting all this stuff to the car."

"I don't need any help. I'm stronger than ever, remember?"

"You may be a new vampire but it doesn't mean you can't tire yourself out. Besides, you should be resting. Next time you'd like to go out, I insist on going with you." Marco leaned his forehead against his wife's.

She touched Marco's face. "You worry too much."

"I would die if anything were to happen to you," Marco threw her packages to the floor and pulled Maggie into his arms, his mouth descending on hers before she could protest.

Dante felt like an intruder spying on their intimacy. Though he tried to suppress it, the twinge of envy squeezed his heart at seeing them carry on as if he weren't in the room. From the moment Maggie walked into the house, his entire body tingled with awareness. And he hated that he couldn't shake these feelings for her. She belonged to Marco, a thing he'd never dare challenge, but it was frustrating nonetheless to wants another vampire's bloodmate. It wasn't supposed to be possible.

Dante had thought long and hard about his emotions, and the only explanation he could come up with was that Maggie had been the first woman he'd shared a deep connection with in a long time. Maggie wasn't just a convenient woman to fuck and forget—she was special. But she was his brother's wife.

Hi mouth watered as he watched Marco caress Maggie's smooth brown skin. Dante remember how soft she'd been beneath his touch, and how her eyes had glazed with passion when he'd once had her in his arms. He couldn't forget how her lush frame had pressed lovingly against him. Dante's cock stirred as he relived that moment in his mind.

The two lovers kissed each other as though they had been apart for a couple of years rather than a couple of hours. Dante cleared his throat loud enough to remind them of his presence. GianMarco took his time pulling away from her. He offered his brother a sheepish grin. Maggie looked at him for the first time since her arrival and smiled warmly. "Dante!"

He opened his arms to receive her as she rushed across the room to greet him with her customary hug.

"Dante! I didn't recognize the vehicle outside. When did you get here?" She locked her arms around his neck.

Dante squeezed her tight against him for a moment, then he bent down and lightly brushed her soft lips with his. "It's new. I arrived not too long after you went on your shopping excursion. You're looking well, *piccola*." He brushed her knuckles against his cheek.

"Thank you, you look pretty good yourself." She placed her hands against his chest and gave me a slight shove to break his hold on her. "Excuse me." She rushed out the room without further explanation.

Dante shot Marco a look of alarm.

Marco chuckled. "Don't worry. She's still in her morning sickness phase."

"But it's well past morning."

"Yes. Unfortunately for Maggie it's more like morning, afternoon, and evening sickness. My poor *ciccina*. The *bambino* is giving his mama a hard time already." Marco grinned from ear to ear. The pride was evident in his voice and it cut Dante; he despised himself for being so jealous.

Marco's smile fell as though he sensed the turmoil within his brother. "Dante —"

"Don't say it. It's something I'm dealing with." His self-disgust cut him to the core.

"In time I know this will pass."

Dante shook his head. "It hasn't yet. I think I should go."

"Please don't. Maggie would be disappointed if you left soon."

"No. I don't think it's a good idea for me to stick around. Please give your wife my regards."

Maggie re-entered the room. "Are you leaving so soon?"

Marco frowned "Maggie, are you okay? That was quick."

"False alarm. Dante, did I overhear you say you're leaving? Don't even think about it, at least not until I cook you a proper meal. I'll make smothered chicken. I remember how much you enjoyed it the last time I made it. I can whip up an apple raspberry pie for dessert." When she looked at him with her big brown eyes and dimpled smile, he could refuse her nothing.

"That sounds delicious. I guess I could stay for a meal. I appreciate the invitation."

She waved her hand dismissively. "You're family, you don't need an invitation. Let me put some of these boxes away and I'll start dinner." As she turned away, Maggie wobbled and nearly lost her balance. He and Marco were at her side in an instant, each of them holding an elbow. When she grabbed for Marco, Dante let go.

"I think it's time for your feeding," Marco said, holding her steady.

"But I fed before I went shopping"

"And you need to do so again. You're a new vampire which means you need to feed often and even more so because you're pregnant.

She nodded. "You're right. I felt dizzy all of a sudden. I've been a vampire for two months and I still haven't gotten used to this." She laughed softly.

Marco lifted her into his arms and she buried her face in his neck.

"Perhaps I'll take a rain check on dinner." Dante began to glide toward the door.

Maggie lifted her head. "Don't go. We won't be long."

He shook his head firmly. He didn't think he'd be able to bear hearing the two of them carry on. "No, you need some privacy. I was just passing through anyway."

"We'll be quick," Marco reaffirmed.

Dante tried to inject a humor into the situation even though it was killing him. "When have you two been quick about a feeding?"

Marco glanced down at Maggie and, although his brother's thoughts were blocked to him, Dante knew he was communicating with her telepathically. Maggie's gaze darted in his direction. Her brow was furrowed she nibbled her bottom lip in apprehension.

"Dante ... maybe ... you would like to take part in my feeding?" she asked shyly.

Dante took a step backward. His eyes widened and he couldn't hold back his surprise. Marco had to have put her up to asking him. Dante was sure Maggie cared for him, but not the same way he did for her.

"No, I couldn't." His eyes locked with his brother's as he touched his mind. *I can't. You know how I feel.*

*I know you want to,* Marco shot back. *It's just a feeding. Besides, I trust you. The extra nourishment will be good for her.*

"Join us," Maggie whispered.

Dante's gaze drifted to her lips. Her eyes strayed to his cock, which was now straining painfully against his pants. He sighed. This was a fight he knew he couldn't win.

As though sensing his acquiescence, Marco turned around and carried Maggie up the stairs. Dante followed.

He watched as Marco laid Maggie on the bed and began undressing himself. Dante unbutton his shirt with trembling fingers, his eyes never leaving her quivering body. Her focus for the most part remained on Marco. Dante told himself to walk away—but he couldn't. Maybe all he needed was to bury himself between her supple thighs just once more and this unholy feeling he had for her would vanish.

His cock ached from wanting her. He licked his dry lips in anticipation of what was to come. When Marco was nude, he began to undress Maggie, kissing the flesh he exposed. "I never get tired of taking your clothes off," he whispered to his wife.

Dante stood naked, watching them as he stroked his dick. He took in every inch of Maggie's bare body. She looked like a voluptuous chocolate goddess. Her large, round breasts were crowned with huge nipples that were so dark they were almost black. They looked so suckable it made his mouth water, and he desperately wanted to taste them. The tangy scent of her pussy drifted to his nostrils and he could no longer stand idle. He walked over to the bed to join them.

Maggie tore her eyes away from Marco and gave Dante a tentative smile. It was all the encouragement he needed. He pulled her away from his brother and wrapped his arms around her, burying his face in her neck and inhaling deeply. He felt her incisors sink into the tender flesh between his shoulder and neck.

Dante thought he would explode from the erotic sensation of her feeding so hungrily. Maggie's breasts crushed against his chest were nearly more than he could take.

Marco leaned forward to form a trail of kisses down her back. Dante held her head tightly against him. "That's enough, *piccola,*" he whispered to her. She lifted her head reluctantly. A drop of his blood ran down the corner of her mouth to her chin. Dante leaned over and licked the trail of blood from her face, causing Maggie to shiver.

"Mmm, that was delicious, Dante, but I want more." Her sensual lips pouted.

Dante felt his balls tighten. How he ached for this woman—a woman who didn't belong to him. She pushed him down on the bed and slid her body down the length of his. He cried out at the friction her skin created against his. She licked her lips, eyeing his cock with a hungry gleam. Her lips brushed against the swollen head of his rock-hard shaft.

Marco grabbed her hips and positioned her on her knees before plunging into her. The rush of Maggie's warm breath against Dante's cock made it so rigid it was near pain. She wrapped her fingers around him and licked the drop of pre-cum that dripped from him. "This is so good. It's been a while since I've been fed from you," she murmured before taking him fully into her mouth.

Dante moaned in pleasure as her lips slid down the length of his shaft. She attacked his member, trying to cram as much of his cock into her mouth as she could. Her body shuddered over his as Marco pounded into her from behind—even as her mouth moved up and down on his dick. She sucked him so deeply that she came close to swallowing him whole. Her mouth moved over him with a wild hunger that sent shockwaves of pleasure rippling through his body.

Dante reached out to bury his fingers into her thick, soft hair. The decadent feeling of her lips bobbing up and down on him was heady, but he secretly craved to sink his dick inside her slick, tight pussy. "*Dio*, Maggie. I don't know if I can control myself when you do that to me." He threw his head back and closed his eyes.

If he blocked out he sounds of Marco's moans, Dante could almost pretend he and Maggie were alone in the room. However, deep down he realized the soft moans vibrating around his cock weren't for him, but for Marco who slammed in and out of her. For a fleeting moment, Dante wished that it was his cock that made her moan so deliciously, and his name that she cried out. He could almost imagine she belonged to him alone and not his brother.

Even as that dangerous thought invaded his mind, he quickly dispelled it. Thinking along those lines would lead to no good. Dante had to keep telling himself Maggie belonged to Marco and that was that.

Maggie gently cupped his balls in her palm and rubbed her thumb against the sensitive skin. Dante's breath caught in his throat at the deliberate touch of her caress. Her free hand worked in motion with her mouth, pumping him, stroking him, and carrying him to an insanely intense peak.

"Maggie!" Dante cried out her name as his seed shot into her mouth.

She made loud slurping noises as she eagerly sucked him dry. She squeezed his highly sensitive balls, milking him of every drop of his essence. Maggie lifted her head and shuddered against him, signaling her own orgasm.

"GianMarco!" she screamed. Maggie collapsed and rested her head against Dante's belly.

Marco pulled out and took Maggie into his arms. A satisfied smile spread across her dark face as she turned to welcome Marco's embrace.

An irrational sense of jealously ripped through Dante and he spun her roughly to face him. He grabbed a handful of her hair before his mouth crashed down on hers. She whimpered under the pressure of his insistent kiss. Maggie pushed at his chest, but her strength did not come close to matching his and he was determined to have her.

She managed to twist her head away from his. Her eyes were wide with bewilderment. "Dante, no!"

Marco pulled them apart, his amber eyes glowing with fury. "What the fuck is wrong with you, Dante?"

Dante loosened his grip on Maggie, and she scrambled away from him. Fear and anger stamped her face, and those were the last emotions he ever wanted her to feel toward him. What had he done? He knew it would be a bad idea to join him but she was his weakness.

"I was only supposed to be a feeding. I thought..." Marco's voice trailed off. He stared at Dante as if he were looking at a stranger. It was more than Dante could take.

"Yes, you were feeling sorry for me, so you decided to throw me a bone." Dante got off the bed and quickly threw his clothing on. "We shouldn't have done this. I have to leave."

Marco touched his mind. *Don't go like this. What just happened?*

*It's no good. This thing I have for her ... I don't understand. She is your bloodmate, yet ... I'm sorry.*

*I don't understand either. I didn't think it possible for a vampire to have more than one bloodmate.*

*It isn't, but ... Dio! I don't know what's wrong with me.*

*Maybe —*

*Please don't try to analyze it.*

*When will we see you again?*

*I don't know. I have a lead in Germany I must investigate. Perhaps when I'm back in the States I'll visit ... with Maggie's permission, of course.*

To his surprise, Maggie slid off the bed. She grabbed her clothes and held it against her body. "Dante, if you could just give me a minute to get dressed, I'd like for you to wait for me outside."

He wasn't sure what she had to say to him but if Maggie told him to never come back, it was no more than he deserved. He looked to his brother who shrugged.

Dante bowed his head in acquiescence. "Okay."

He only had to wait a few moments before Maggie joined him in the living room, fully dressed. There was a caution in her step that had never been there before. At least not with him.

She offered him a tentative smile. "Dante."

The awkwardness of the moment broke his heart. The ease in which they used to communicate was absent. "Marco isn't joining us?"

"He's taking a quick shower. It's okay because I wanted to speak with you in private."

"Look, I'm sorry —"

She held up her hand to cut him off. "There's no need to apologize. I just wanted you to know I'm not angry with you, I was just caught off guard is all. I'm still new to the ways of vampire protocol, but what happened in there was more than just a feeding to you, wasn't it? I mean, I understand that the act itself is supposed to be pleasurable but I felt that a line was somehow crossed."

Dante bowed his head in shame. "I understand if I'm no longer welcome here."

Maggie surprised him again by stepping closer and gently taking his face in her palms. "Promise me you won't beat yourself up over this. You mean a lot to GianMarco and it would disappoint him if you kept yourself in exile."

"And you? How do you feel?" He had to be a glutton for punishment to ask her a question he already knew the answer to.

"I care about you too. We're family. I-I love you. My feelings for you are probably stronger than the ones I feel for Niccolo and Romeo but I suspect it's because of how strongly you're connected to GianMarco. I'm *in* love with him. He's my bloodmate. Do you understand?"

Dante nodded, not trusting himself to speak. It was the old "I love you but I'm not in love with you" speech. He'd chuckled when he'd seen it played over and over again between the humans he sometimes observed. He never thought he'd be on the receiving end of this speech, or that it would hurt so goddamn much.

"And I don't believe you're in love with me either, Dante. You might think you are but after a little introspection I'm sure you'll come to that realization as well." She stood on the tips of her toes to plant a light peck on his lips. That little kiss, though it meant nothing more than a gesture of comfort to her, it meant the world to him.

She pulled away from him then and dropped her arms to her sides. "In the meantime, don't stay away too long. GianMarco needs you. We both do. And don't even think about depriving your niece of her uncle."

For the first time, Dante smiled. "Niece? You seem so sure."

Maggie touched her stomach protectively. "Of course I am. A mother knows these things."

"You couldn't keep me away if you tried."

"Glad to hear it." She wrapped her arms around his waist and gave him a quick embrace. "Take care of yourself, okay?"

"I always do." Unable to help himself he grazed her cheek with his knuckles. "Goodbye, Maggie."

"Bye," she whispered.

As Dante walked out of the house, he didn't dare turn back because he didn't think he could bare the sight of Maggie right now. The worst part wasn't that she didn't return his feelings, he'd known all along she never would. It was her pity.

## Chapter Three

Sasha walked up to the door of the imposing manor with a sense of impending doom. Even though she was ninety-nine, the thought of having a conversation with her father gave her a nervous feeling in the pit of her stomach. The door opened before she knocked. Dmitri Bolshoy, the family butler, stood at the door, his face dour and his demeanor stiff.

"Miss Romanova, your father is expecting you." He opened the door, allowing her entry. She barely felt the tingle of her father's protective wards as she walked over the threshold. The old conquered warlock's lip curled slightly. It was enough to demonstrate his resentfulness without being blatantly disrespectful. All of the servants at the Romanov compound held the same gleam of defiance and anger in their eyes. Sasha suspected that if she had been conquered she, too, would resent being forced into servitude by the one who was responsible for that fate.

Long before Sasha had been born, witches and warlocks would challenge one another to a battle of power in order to become more powerful and to establish supremacy. When a witch or warlock was killed by another of their kind, some of their power was absorbed by the killer. In the case of challenges, the victor agreed to spare the defeated party's life in order to absorb enough power to render their opponent powerless. However, there was often a gross mismatch— despite the fact that witches and warlocks possessed the same basic skills and all received similar training, each also possessed their own special talents. A warlock whose main power was levitation for instance was no match for another witch or warlock who was a conjurer. The losers became "conquered" and had to serve the victors for three centuries; they were no better than slaves and Sasha felt sorry for them.

The practice was not so common now as it had been, but her father had won so many challenges over the years that he still had many servants. Sasha was glad this barbaric practice was practically nonexistent now.

Being born a witch or a warlock guaranteed immortality to the extent that one never died from natural causes, but there was a price to pay. Not unlike rogue vampires, there were witches and warlocks like her father who craved more power, and stopped at nothing to claim another's power by fair means or foul. There were even those who were not true immortals and stayed alive solely by practicing black magic. They were called the dark ones.

She gave the butler a sympathetic smile before walking past him, then took another deep breath as she made her way to her father's study. Sasha would have turned back around if this weren't so important to her.

Her son was missing.

Her brothers were on a sojourn, unable to be reached, and Niccolo ... well, if she could find Jagger through other means she didn't want to worry Niccolo before she deemed it necessary.

She entered the study to find her father, his back turned to her, looking out the window. "So you've come crawling back, wanting my help. It figures." Ivan Romanov's deep voice echoed throughout the room even though he barely spoke above a whisper.

Sasha moistened her parched lips before she answered. As always her father's words were blunt and cutting. "Papa, can't you for once put aside your dislike of me? I'm sure you already know that my son, your grandson, is missing. Please tell me where I can find him."

Ivan turned around; his sky-blue eyes, so unlike her own, glittered with an emotion she couldn't read. A malevolent smile spread across his face. Her father was nearly six hundred. With his aristocratic features and thick platinum-blond locks that cascaded past his shoulder, he didn't look a day over forty in a human's life span. He stood just over six feet and had a stocky build. He would have been quite handsome were it not for the harsh stamp of arrogance he seemed to wear with pride. "So you come here as my daughter now? Were you not the one who left the protection of our coven?"

She balled her fists at her sides. "Only after you made it impossible for me to stay."

He raised a blond brow. "I?"

"Yes, you. You've made it clear from the day I was born how disappointing I am to you. Your constant need to control everyone was suffocating. I dealt with it most of my life but I refused to subject my son to that."

"You dare stand there and criticize the way I run my family when it is you who turned my sons against me? Your sister is dead because you are a poor excuse for a witch. Despite that, I didn't force you to leave. That was your choice."

"Papa, no matter what you think, I'm not stupid. You might not say it in words, but your every look conveys how you feel. When I went to you and Mama to tell you I was carrying a child I needed you love and support, but you turned your backs on me. There was no telling how you would have treated any offspring of mine."

"Sasha, I would never have treated Nikolai badly. He is my grandson." Ivan popped in front of her before she could respond and lightly caressed her cheek. Her father had never been a demonstrative man. She wondered if this was his way of trying to cross the chasm between them.

For a moment she wanted to believe him. All her life, all she ever wanted from her father was his love. Her eyes moistened with tears. "You wouldn't have?" she asked with uncertainty.

"Of course not, child. I would never blame an innocent child just because his mother is a worthless second-rate witch. It's a shame you weren't born human. At least you'd be dead by now."

She cried out, backing away from him. If he had slapped her it wouldn't have hurt as much. Her father had a way of cutting her to the core without batting an eye. He'd said hurtful things to her in his lifetime but this was by far the worst. Her insides felt as though they'd been ripped by sharp razors.

She wanted nothing more than to turn around, walk out the door and never step foot in this house again. But she swallowed her pride for the sake of her son. She had to find out Jagger's whereabouts.

Ivan chuckled, seeming amused at the pain he'd caused. "I see you no longer lose that temper of yours so easily. Perhaps you accept my words as the truth."

She squeezed her eyes shut and silently counted to ten. She wouldn't let him push her buttons. Not this time. "I don't care what you think about me, but I am begging you to invoke the search chant and find my son."

Ivan wasn't finished taunting her, however. "Why don't you ask your brothers? Maybe they'll help you,"

"You know they are away. If you won't help me, perhaps I can ask Mama. Where is she?" Sasha and her mother were not close either, but there was more compassion in Maria Romanova's heart than her husband's.

"Visiting relatives. You give up too easily."

"What is it that you want from me? Do you want me to beg some more? Fine! I beg you. Please help me find my son. If you won't invoke the chant, release me, and I'll do it myself. Please, Papa." She hastily wiped away an angry tear.

Ivan studied her with a cool expression. He folded his arms. "He is a Romanov. He'll be fine. Let him be a man for once."

"What are saying?" she demanded.

"You've coddled that boy. It's about time Jagger develops a set of balls."

"He's gone looking for his father. Do you know what will happen once he starts asking around about him?"

"No one would dare touch my grandson. I know —" He broke off.

Sasha narrowed her eyes. "What do you know?"

"I know the most important thing of course; anyone would be a fool to touch a Romanov."

"I see. So you won't help me."

He snorted. "It would be a waste of time."

"Because he's my son? Is it because he's so important to me that you don't give a damn?"

"You will not take that tone with me in my home, young woman. I am still your father and I demand your respect under my roof!"

"When have you done anything to earn my respect? For years, I wondered what I could do to make you as proud of me as you are of my brothers and to make you love me the way you did Petra."

"I —"

She shook her head as tears stung her eyes. "I don't care what you say anymore. I came to you because I thought maybe, just maybe, you have some feeling for your grandson, but as usual, I am wasting my time. Don't worry, *Ivan*, I will never darken your doorstep again." She turned to leave, but he teleported in front of her, blocking the door.

"Sasha —"

"I don't want to hear it. Please move."

Her father's face was bright red. "You will not walk away from me."

"Oh? What are you doing to do to me if I do? I have nothing left for you to take. I won't stick around to take more of your abuse. Now excuse me, I must go look for my son. *Do svidanya, Ivan.*" She pushed past him.

Now that she knew she couldn't count on her father, there was only one person she could turn to ... Niccolo.

<><><>

"Open your legs a little wider, darling." Niccolo buried his face between Linda's thighs.

She moaned with delight. "Oh, baby, yeah. You eat pussy so well."

He glided his tongue against her clit and slid his fingers into her damp heat. Linda had been the woman whom he and Romeo had spied on the dance floor a few days earlier. She'd come to the club the next night, and again tonight. Her seductive dance movements were tempting enough for him to offer her an invitation to his office for a private party, which she'd eagerly accepted.

After a quick fuck against a wall in his office, she suggested going back to her place for an all-nighter. It had been a few weeks since he had fed and Linda seemed ready for action. Which lead him to this moment, feasting on her pussy.

Niccolo fastened his lips over her clit, sucking roughly, creating just enough pressure to make her writhe uncontrollably beneath him. She screamed. "Oh, God, you're going to be the death of me!"

Niccolo lifted his head and gave her a slight small. "But it's the best kind of death, isn't it?"

"Oh, yeah," she moaned, grinding her pussy against his face, seeming unable to get enough of his mouth and tongue. He licked her from her clit to the crack of her ass. Linda stiffened beneath the ministrations of his tongue as he fed, hungrily slurping the nectar from her cunt.

Her fingers dug into his hair as she moaned and sighed deep in her throat. He licked her labia, making sure he got every drop of her honey. Niccolo lifted his head to see her staring down at him with passion-glazed eyes. He knew he could bring her to another orgasm in minutes if he really wanted to, but, strangely, he didn't.

Niccolo couldn't shake an ominous feeling that something wasn't quite right. He slid up next to the now-still Linda and placed a gentle kiss on her thin but inviting lips. "Thank you, Linda."

"Are you going to ... I mean, don't you want to finish?"

"Umm ..." Without hurting her feelings, how could he tell her that he no longer had the inclination to finish fucking her? To be honest, now he wasn't quite sure why he had approached her in the first place.

Actually he did know but refused to acknowledge it.

Shit! As he glanced at Linda, all he could think of was Sasha. It didn't help matters that Linda had dark hair and eyes, and skin so pale it was like cream, just like Sasha's. "I'm sorry, Linda." He kissed her again.

She pouted. "That quickie back at the club doesn't count. I wants some more of your big, beautiful cock."

He climbed out of bed and began to dress. "I'm sorry, but I have to go. Forgive me."

"You're really leaving?" she asked incredulously, as though it were inconceivable that a man could walk away from her. Niccolo knew her type well— a good time party girl looking to find the next sucker to finance her lifestyle of more partying, boozing, and drugging. He had, in fact, tasted faint traces of cocaine and ecstasy in her secretions. Though she would have willingly given him some more pussy, he knew it would be wiser to leave her alone.

He didn't need any more complications in his life. Damn, times like these he wished he could be as outspoken as Romeo, who would know how to easily extricate himself from this situation. "I'm sorry, *bellisima*, but I have some pressing matters to take care of."

"So all you wanted to do was eat my pussy? Well, at least let me reciprocate. I'm not sure all of that big dick will fit in my mouth, but I can try." She grinned at him and moved off the bed to stand in front of him. She rubbed her small breasts against his arm.

"I'm sorry, but I really do have to leave." He gently pushed her away and quickly donned the rest of his clothes as Linda watched in obvious disbelief.

She crossed her arms and scowled at him. "What's wrong with you? Are you a fag or something?" She didn't look so pretty anymore, and he was no longer interested in sparing her feelings.

"If that was meant to be an insult I've been called far worse. To be quite honest, Linda, I'm no longer interested." He grasped her chin between his thumb and index finger, forcing her to meet his stare. "Get your life together, stay off the drugs and never come to my club again."

She nodded in a daze at his hypnotic suggestions. He rarely glamoured humans but Linda was the persistent type.

Once he was sure she'd taken his suggestions to heart, he released her chin.

"*Ciao, bellisima.*" He left the room before she could respond. He had been a fool to go there in the first place.

With his Linda problem resolved, he wished he could shake off the feeling of impending doom. He couldn't figure out why something just seemed off.

Niccolo slid into his black Ferrari and started the engine. He debated whether to head back to the club or not and decided against it. His business manager would make sure things were running smoothly, and it wasn't like he couldn't use the rest. He tried to empty his mind as he drove through downtown L.A.

He couldn't help but think about the events of the past couple of months. He had been an agent in the Underground since it had been formed, by his eldest brother, Dante. It had been created to eliminate the rogue vampire threat. Dante's main goal however, was to find the one called *Il Diavolo*, the rogue Dante believed was responsible for the murder of their parents. Things of late were coming to a head, and yet this was the first week that he was not on an assignment for the Underground.

He pulled up to a gated Beverly Hills condo community and stopped at the security post.

"Good evening, Mr. Grimaldi."

"Good evening, Thomas."

The security guard, Thomas, was usually very chatty. Normally, Niccolo would not have minded sparing a few moments to talk to the obviously bored man, but tonight was not one of those times.

"I see you took the Ferrari out tonight. On a nice night like this, I would have thought you'd take out the Porsche so you could drive with the top down."

"Is it nice out? I didn't notice. I have several things to attend to, so I'm in a bit of a hurry tonight. Would you open the gate, please?"

Thomas looked a little taken aback by his abruptness but opened the gate. "Sure thing, Mr. Grimaldi. Have a nice night," he said, sounding a bit put out. Niccolo decided to make it up to him later.

"Oh, wait!"

Niccolo stopped his car and looked back.

"A pretty young lady came by looking for you, but I couldn't let her in, you know. Security reasons and all."

Niccolo nodded and thanked the guard. What else was new? There were always women trying to get into his home.

He pulled into his parking spot and got out of the car. As he approached his condo, his sixth sense went crazy. Someone was inside his home; he could hear them pacing in his living room. Rogue? He took a deep whiff of the night air. No, it wasn't another vampire, but he didn't think it was a human either.

His fingers shifted to claw-like talons, and his incisors descended. Whoever had gotten inside his home was about to get gutted. He treaded lightly as he made his way to the door, and pressed his ear against the door. The pacing back and forth on his carpeted floor continued. It seemed like someone was waiting for him. Wanting to keep the element of surprise on his side, he burst through the door ready to strike.

When he saw who was on the other side of the door, it was he who was stunned. His wide-eyed visitor was none other than Sasha Romanova.

"Thank God you're home," she cried before catapulting herself into his arms.

## Chapter Four

"Sasha!" He wrapped his arms around her slight frame to hold her steady. His mind went numb as a flash flood of emotions coursed through him. Seeing her again so suddenly brought back painful memories he had tried to put behind him. Niccolo often regretted the way they had last parted.

The first time he'd met Sasha while visiting her family over thirty years ago, they had gotten along well. He had admired her serenity, her quirky sense of humor, and the way her expressive eyes grew animated whenever she spoke. She wasn't the kind person who only talked to hear themselves speak. When Sasha spoke her words her conversation was interesting and insightful. Once he had met Petra, however, Sasha had somehow faded into the background. The odd thing was, besides that night when they'd made Jagger, and their last confrontation, he couldn't remember much else about their interactions.

Sasha had not reached out to him since, and the only reason why he could think she could not was because of something pertaining to his son. His heart began to race out of control. He gripped her forearms and held her away from him so that he could see her face. "Where's Jagger?"

Sasha's eyes were red, and the dark circles around them indicated she had not gotten a decent night's sleep for a while. "I had hoped he was with you. Oh, God, he's been gone for nearly a week now!" She broke off on a sob.

He furrowed his brow. "Why wasn't I notified sooner? Why did you allow him to venture out on his own?"

Her bottom lip trembled and she looked as if she were on the verge of breaking down again. "You make him sound like a child. He's a man now and free to come and go as he pleases."

"Then why are you so worried?"

"Because I feel that something has happened to him. We talk nearly every day. When I didn't hear from him for a few days, I knew something was wrong. I went by his apartment and from the looks of things, he hadn't been there in a while. The last time we spoke, he was upset. He ... he wanted to know about you."

"This is the first time he has asked about me?" A searing pain lanced through Niccolo's body. It hurt like hell to know that while he thought about Jagger daily, his son gave him little thought. His eyes narrowed. "What did you tell him about me?"

"Don't give me that look. I've never spoken a word against you. I told him who you were. He was shocked to learn of his powerful connections. I'd congratulate you, but you already know you and your brothers are quite famous in the immortal circles."

"Sasha, your sarcasm isn't helping matters."

She sighed. "You're right. I'm a bit stressed right now. May I sit down?"

"Since you've already found your way into my home, you should have made yourself comfortable. Did you teleport inside?"

"No. Actually your cleaning lady left the door slightly ajar when she was bringing her cleaning supplies from her vehicle. I hid while she cleaned."

"If you didn't use your powers to get in, how did you get past the guard?"

"He turned me away at first, but this older couple who lives here apparently saw me and asked me why I looked so distressed. I told them I wanted to surprise my brother with a visit and we hadn't seen each other for a long time. They vouched for me with the security guard." She sounded quite pleased with herself.

"What? No magic? You always seem to use that to get what you want," he taunted.

Her face turned bright red. "I know what you're implying. However, as you've pointed out, you don't need my sarcasm, so I certainly don't need your nasty innuendoes."

She was right. The most important thing right now was discovering Jagger's whereabouts.

"Are you positive he's missing? Maybe he just needed to get away for a few days to think things through."

"No. He wouldn't go away without letting me know. He knows how I worry about him. There's something else happening here."

"What?"

"I think he wants to be more in tune with his vampire side. He was asking me questions I couldn't answer."

"Well, has he had his first taste of blood?"

She frowned. "I don't know but if he hasn't I'm to blame. I never encouraged him to explore his vampire side. But he never brought up until a week ago. I'm scared for him; he's not quite thirty and still hasn't fully grasped the mechanics of his powers."

Niccolo tried to think of what all this could mean. Vampires needed to feed, and though Jagger was only half vampire, it didn't make the need any less. The consequences of a full blood not feeding were dire but he wasn't sure how that would affect his son. "Why have you not allowed him to learn of his vampire traits?"

"I thought if he suppressed that side of him, it would decrease the likelihood of him being tracked down by your enemies. I wish I'd done things differently. I fear I've left him vulnerable to..." she covered her mouth to hold back a muffled cry.

"There's something you're not telling me."

"The night he came to me, he seemed ... sick."

"Sick? We can't get sick unless ... what were the symptoms?"

"There was a reddish tint to his eyes. His skin looked a little on the pink side as well, like he were feverish. He felt warm to the touch. I didn't really know what to make of it. I was too busy trying to comfort him."

"*Dio!* We must find him soon."

A look of panic crossed her face. "What is it? Tell me, please!"

"Our son, he needs to feed."

"But he has been with women. They practically throw themselves at him." Confusion was written all over her pretty but tired face. Her lips were still the deep red he remembered, and her skin was still like cream. He had the strongest urge to take her into his arms and sample those tasty-looking lips. Niccolo wanted to slowly strip her of each article of clothing.

This was complete madness! His son was missing and possibly in danger, but all he could thing about was burying his cock so deep in her pussy he wouldn't know where he ended and she began. Damn Sasha for making his body react this way to her. "*Strega*," he muttered.

"Calling me a witch isn't much of an insult since I am one. If there's something happening to Jagger that you're aware of, please tell me."

Niccolo raked his fingers through his hair. She frustrated the hell out of him, pretending as though she hadn't bewitched him. There could be no other explanation of why he was this way around her. Once he was assured that his son was safe, he would demand that she release him from this spell or, so help her lovely little neck, he would break her in two.

"Jagger may have been with many women as you've said, and the probability is quite high that he had fed from their essence. As a matter of fact, he must have, otherwise he'd be in way worse shape by now. Those sexual secretions probably served as some form of relief but they can't sustain him forever. He needs his first blood."

"But he's only half vampire. I never thought it was necessary for him to do that."

"He's vampire enough to need blood and if he hasn't had blood in nearly thirty years, he's in trouble. He's still young, a baby among our kind, so his needs to feed often. If he doesn't that could be dangerous. His being a hybrid might have worked in his favor, however. It's probably kept him together all these years."

"So all we need to do if find make sure he gets his first blood."

"It's not that simple. When a vampire is born or made, they need first blood from a close blood tie—me or you, for example. From what you've described, he's in the beginning stages of *la morte dolci*. It's very possible if we don't track him down, innocent blood may be shed."

"No! He would never hurt anyone!"

"He might not want to, but once *la morte dolci* takes hold of him, he may not be able to control himself. Why didn't you invoke some kind of spell to find him? You're good at casting spells."

She shoved him as her dark eyes flashed fire. "I won't take any more of your veiled comments! Don't you think if I could have, I would have? Now, will you help me locate him or not?" She looked even prettier when she was angry.

Niccolo shook his head to rid himself of his carnal thoughts. Wait a minute. She'd said she couldn't cast a spell. It was on the tip of his tongue to ask why when his cell phone began to vibrate.

He dug it out from his breast pocket. "Niccolo speaking."

"Nico, it's Dante. We have a situation in Munich. How soon can you get over here?"

Niccolo took a deep breath. This was the last thing he needed. He didn't mind going on missions for the Underground, but there were times like these when he wished he had never heard the name *Il Diavolo.* "Dante, I've never turned you down when you needed me, but I have a bit of a situation here myself."

"What's that problem? If it's some woman then I'm sure she'll wait for you when you return. I need you here."

Niccolo found it a bit insulting his brother would think he'd allow just any random woman to get between him and family business. "You know me better than that, Dante."

Dante released a heavy sigh. "You're right. I apologize. I'm a bit stressed. What's happening on your end?"

"Sasha is here, and Jagger is missing."

"Are you fucking kidding me? This is worse than I thought. If Sasha's with you then you both need to get over here."

What the hell? What in the world was his brother talking about? "Why?"

"Because I think your son has been through here."

"What? Have you seen him? Where is he?"

Sasha's eyes widened with fear. "Is it Jagger? Has something happened to my baby?"

Niccolo held up his hand to silence her as he listened to Dante.

"There has been rogue activity over here and the bloodshed has been monumental."

"Have any Underground agents been lost?" Niccolo asked.

"No ... all of the dead are human. Rogues usually leave humans alone, but this — God, Nico, there were children here. The media is all over this, calling it some satanic ritual gone awry. But this massacre could only have been perpetuated by our kind."

"Why would you think my son was involved?"

"The minute I got near the scene, I picked up what I believed was your scent at first but as I lingered I noticed a subtle difference. I couldn't figure out why I was picking it up since you're obviously in L.A., but now that you say Jagger is missing ..."

"My son is not a rogue!"

"Calm down, Nico. I'm not saying he is. I only said that I think he's been through here."

"Tell me this isn't happening. Dante ... he hasn't tasted first blood yet."

"Are you sure?"

"According to Sasha, he has not. She says the last time she saw him, he was warm and looked a little sick."

"*La morte dolci,*" Dante groaned the words. "What were the other symptoms?"

Niccolo explained while his brother listened silently on the other end of the line.

Sasha looked at him with an anxious expression on her face. Her lips were pressed so tightly together they lost all color. He wanted to wrap her within his embrace to reassure her everything would be okay. But who would reassure him?

"You're in Munich?" Niccolo asked.

"Yes. We're staying at Wolf's. Romeo is here, as well as Angel and Carter."

"Okay. We'll be there. I'll text you our flight schedule and call when we land at the airport."

"I'll have a car waiting for you."

Niccolo disconnected.

"What is it?" Sasha asked anxiously.

"That was Dante. He believes that Jagger may be or may have been in Germany recently."

"And?"

"And he may have been involved in some kind of slaughter."

"Slaughter? He's wrong. Jagger wouldn't hurt anyone. Why would your brother say these awful things?"

"Dante didn't say he was, just that he's somehow connected. But I too refuse to believe that Jagger is capable of such atrocities. But if he's in the throes of *la morte dolci,* he may not be able to help himself."

"No." Sasha shook her head vehemently. "Even then, I don't believe it."

"From what you said, he might still be in the early stages of the illness, so it isn't likely he would do such a thing even if he were capable of it."

"Yet." She said aloud what was on his mind.

"Let's not think about this right now. It's quite possible that he went to spend some time on his own." He hoped.

"You're not leaving anything out, are you? This ailment you speak of is foreign to me. I need you to explain it to me so I can understand what Jagger might be going through."

Niccolo sighed. He didn't want to waste time explaining *la morte dolci*, when they needed to get going, but as his son's mother she had the right to know.

"It's very complicated. The simplest way to explain it is that when a vampire is denied something that he needs, blood or a mate, for example, it can drive him into the state we call *la morte dolci*. I have not personally experienced it, but my brother GianMarco did when he denied himself his bloodmate. To hear him explain the illness, it made him feverish and caused him a great deal of physical pain. His bodily functions were out of control and his temperature rose to scorching proportions. My brother was in such bad shape that he lost all rational thought and attacked his bloodmate, who had been human at the time. Had Dante not intervened, he might have killed her."

"Oh, no!" Sasha covered her mouth in horror. "The poor woman must have been frightened out of her mind."

"I'm sure she was. I wasn't there."

"But how did he get past this illness?"

"He stopped denying himself and took what he wanted."

"And his bloodmate? Is she okay?"

"Better than okay. They're married now and expecting their first child together. My new sister is sure that the baby will be a girl, but she may be in for a little disappointment; female-born vampires are quite rare." He smiled briefly as he thought of the happiness his younger brother had found with Maggie. Marco deserved a little happiness after the brutal slaughter of his first wife and child long ago.

"I'm glad that things worked out for them."

"So am I." He glanced at his watch and mentally calculated how long it would take them to get to the airport. "We have to get to Jagger soon. We have to leave now."

She nodded. "This is my fault. I wanted so badly to protect him; I might have done more harm than good."

"There's no point in beating yourself up over it."

"But I kept so much from him. I kept his true birth certificate hidden in case someone within the immortal network was to discover it. Your family isn't the only one with enemies. My father has made many over the centuries. We didn't mingle with other immortals beside my brothers. From the time he was very young I told him to never reveal his powers around anyone but myself and his uncles."

"You made him suppress his warlock side as well?"

"Only around humans. He still received his training under Blade."

"So your father had nothing to do with him even though it's customary for the heads of your covens to train young witches and warlocks?"

"Yes, but the last thing I wanted was for my child to be subjected to my father's demands of perfection. Ivan had a way of making one feel inadequate for the slightest of flaws. And after what happened to Petra ... well, we barely spoke. Even as a baby, Jagger was very smart. He would have picked up on our tenuous relationship."

"I understand." Niccolo could sense her pain and knew she had suffered, but he felt so conflicted. One second, he wanted to hate her; the next moment, he wanted to hold her and promise everything would be okay.

"Sasha, you could have come to me at anytime for help."

"We agreed it was best not to keep in touch. But had I known how suppressing his nature would put him in such a precarious position, I would have reached out sooner. But let me ask you something. What about me, Niccolo? If *I* needed you, would you have come?"

Her question caught him off guard so he hesitated to answer. "I…" He was at a loss for words. Would he have gone to her?

Niccolo wanted to punch himself when he saw the sad droop to her lips. She slowly shook her heads. "Don't bother. I already know the answer. Like you said, we have to get out of here. Let's go."

They were silent for most of the ride to the airport. Niccolo wanted to say something, anything, to take that haunted look from her eyes and to ease the awkward tension between them. "I'm surprised that your brother would defy your father and train Jagger. I'm sure Ivan wasn't pleased."

It took a moment for Sasha to respond. "No," she said quietly, "he wasn't, but my brothers have limited contact with my father. They had a falling out with him as well."

"When and why did this happen?"

"Not too long ago. No one will give a reason, but I think it has something to do with the Council."

Niccolo stiffened at the mention of the Council. "Why do you say that?"

"Something that Cutter let slip. I'm not sure what he meant. My brothers haven't been very forthcoming about the situation, but one night Cutter came over to visit. I think he and Papa had just argued because he was extremely upset. He was evasive when I tried to find out what was going on, but I was eventually able to get some information from him. Cutter said Papa had been plotting for years with a few unsavory characters, but he wouldn't explain. He also said the plot will change life as we know it and that Papa has the Council's backing."

"Did he tell you anything else?"

"No. That was it. It was hard enough getting him to reveal that much. I love my brothers, but they always feel they have to protect me. I know their hearts are in the right place, but it's frustrating at times."

Niccolo had a sneaking suspicion that what was going on with the Council and the massacres were tied together, but he wasn't sure how. He vowed to find out. For now however, the most important was finding his son before it was too late.

## Chapter Five

"Keep up, young one. We should be there shortly."

Although he was faster than any human could ever be, Jagger had a hard time keeping up with the red-haired, older vampire. He felt as though his heart would explode from the exertion. They must have run well over a hundred miles already, but even now he couldn't believe what had happened and what he'd witnessed. Jagger wasn't sure why he continued to follow this vampire, but he felt somehow compelled to do so. He didn't know if it was his quest for answers or some dark force driving him. How in the hell did he get involved in this mess?

It was only a week ago when he had been working at an engineering firm. He had had a comfortable life with no attachments, except a lady friend every now and then whenever the urge took him. His Uncle Blade was training him to unleash the full potential of his powers as a warlock, and he wanted for nothing except to know his father.

His mother had done her best by him. She had filled his life with so much warmth and compassion that he knew he was loved. Maybe she had spoiled him a little, because when he finally took a mate he would want someone with a big heart like her. He didn't consider himself a mama's boy in the traditional sense but there wasn't anyone he was closer to than her. Her unwavering love had enabled him to grow and express himself freely. Still, there had always been a void. One he could no longer ignore. His father.

All his life Jagger had been told his father had loved him very much, but there were never any other details. When he was younger, he hadn't minded so much, but as he grew older, it had become harder to suppress his vampire side, and he had had no one to discuss such matters with.

Jagger had been fifteen when he'd fucked his first woman. The entire time he was with her, he could think of nothing he wanted more than to sink his teeth into her soft flesh. He'd had to settle for feasting on her cunt juice instead. It had soothed him then, but now it was no longer enough.

Although his mother and uncles had answered his questions to the best of their ability, he needed answers about his vampire heritage. And there was only one person who he could turn to. The night he had gone to see his mother, it had felt as if he were burning from the inside out.

After leaving his mother's home, he'd known then what he had to do. It was still hard to believe that his father was a member of the Grimaldi clan, and even harder to comprehend that though he'd been prepared to go to Los Angeles, he was still in Europe. He had already bought his ticket and was waiting in the boarding lounge for his flight when the red-haired vampire approached him. It was how Jagger had ended up in Germany — with his father."

"Here we are, young one." The older vampire gave him a smile that made Jagger a bit uneasy.

Jagger paused. The place looked like an abandoned warehouse, but when he walked inside, it was furnished as grandly as a palace.

"Please make yourself at home."

"This is your home?" Jagger asked with uncertainty.

"Yes. One of them. I have several bases. One must be mobile for what I do."

"I see."

"Would you like a drink, young one? I know you Russians are fond of your vodka. I have the finest bar in all of Europe. Please have a seat; after all, what is mine is yours, of course." There was an unreadable expression in the red-head's amber eyes, and Jagger squirmed in his discomfort. "I sense your unease, young one. Why don't you relax and I'll fix you a drink to soothe your nerves. You have lived too long under your mother's thumb and don't realize the way things are done among our kind, but you will learn." A condescending smile accompanied his words.

"Leave my mother out of this. This is between you and me. Those people back there …they were innocents. Why did you …?" Jagger faltered, unable to take his mind from the slaughter he had witnessed. He knew very well that vampires could be brutal, but the taking of innocent lives was something he didn't understand. It was the act of a rogue, and from the very little he knew of his father, Niccolo Grimaldi was no rogue.

Jagger could still hear the screaming and pleading in his head. The image of a pretty little girl chilled him the most. Her lifeless eyes seemed to ask him why. He cursed himself for not having been able to stop the carnage, for having hungered for their blood. Self-disgust formed in the pit of his belly.

"They were human and of no consequence to us." The vampire shrugged. "Now, have a seat. I will return shortly."

Jagger sat down, still unable to shake his unease. This was not what he had had in mind when he'd gone looking for his father, and he debated getting up and leaving, but his need for answers made him stay where he was.

His host returned shortly with a drink in his hands. "Here. Drink it all. It will make you feel better." The older vampire suddenly frowned and narrowed his eyes. "Where the hell do you think you're going?"

Jagger stiffened but then realized the question wasn't directed toward him.

Seeming to appear from nowhere, a tall, striking woman came into Jagger's line of vision. She easily had one of the most arresting faces he'd ever seen. It was a rare, exotic type of beauty that was capable of leaving many speechless, with her perfectly proportioned features, dark skin and lithe frame. Jagger knew right away she wasn't human. Her face remained blank, but her overly generous lips curled into an almost sneer as she spoke to his host. "Out."

Dark auburn brows furrowed. "Where out?"

"I have things to do." She sounded bored and looked even more so.

"When will you be back?"

"When you see me." She headed toward the exit.

"Nya!"

She halted but she kept her back to him.

"You know what happens if you don't return."

"How can I forget?" And with that she was gone.

Jagger wasn't sure what that exchange was about, but nothing could make this night even more of a nightmare than it already was. "Your lover?"

His host sat back in his chair, his smile returning. "She's not important. Drink."

The beautiful vampire femme forgotten, he took a sip from his glass to steady his nerves. Jagger winced as the alcohol burned a trail down his throat.

The redhead laughed. "I see you are not used to drinking. Personally, alcohol doesn't do a thing for me — one of the drawbacks of being as old as I am — but it does have a soothing effect, doesn't it? Of course, this is obviously your first taste of the stuff. After all, I understand you were thoroughly twisted in your mama's apron strings."

Jagger's eyes narrowed at the taunt. He tilted his head back and gulped the rest of the drink down in one swallow, then slammed the glass defiantly on the end table.

"So you have some spirit, after all. I'm pleased to see that. You might do. Tell me, why did tonight's events bother you so much?"

"Because those people did nothing to deserve what happened to them. You and your men killed them as though you were animals."

"It is what we are. We are the ones who will inherit the Earth. You, more than anyone, should know this. It is a shame your mother hasn't told you."

"Told me what?"

"Well, as you are half warlock and half vampire, you will be very powerful, indeed. One side does not cancel the other out, you know."

"I don't understand what you're getting at." Jagger clutched his head. His thoughts seemed jumbled and cloudy.

"It's very simple. Even though you're not a full blood, you'll still have the same abilities of both sides as you age. You are the future. Imagine what would happen were you to mate with ... a shifter, perhaps. Do you realize how powerful your offspring would be? There would be no stopping our cause then."

"Your cause?" Jagger was confused.

"I see you're still not getting it. No matter. In time you will. Tonight was only the beginning."

"You plan on killing more innocent people?" Jagger asked incredulously. This couldn't be real. He shook his head to alleviate the fuzziness surrounding his thoughts, but he couldn't seem to focus.

"Innocents? You think humans are innocent? For centuries they used up what is rightfully ours. We deserve the right to walk around without suppressing our nature. You especially should feel outraged. How many of your ancestors were burned at the stake in the name of their God, who has long since turned his back on us? Look at you now. You're in pain. I can feel it. Your body temperature is rising and you hunger for something, but you don't know what. You lie awake at night, breaking out in a sweat. You seek out women, but you force yourself to not take what you really want."

"How do you know?"

"How could I not know? It's obvious to me that you are in the beginning stages of *la morte dolci*. I bet your mother and precious uncles never mentioned anything about it, did they? You've been so busy trying to stifle your vampire side that you've been making yourself sick."

Jagger opened his mouth to speak, then immediately closed it. He *had* held a part of himself back but it was mostly to please his mother. Was it possible that her motives in telling him to do so were not as altruistic as he had thought? No. He refused to believe it. "My mother did what she could to protect me."

"No, what she did was handicap you. She knew exactly what she was doing. The tears whenever you asked about your father. The sad little faces. The truth is your mother and uncles manipulated you. You should have been raised among your vampire kin; maybe then you would have realized your full potential."

Jagger's heart clenched in his chest. Everything that the ancient said made an odd kind of sense. A war of emotions flowed through him. He felt angry and defensive at the same time. He was almost positive his mother had never intentionally led him astray, but now he had doubts. "Why would my mother do this? I thought —"

"You think she loves you? I'm sure she does, in her way, but is it really love to keep a father from his son? Your mother used you as a pawn. Can you imagine the pain of someone separated from his child? Oh yes, she knew exactly what she was doing, but enough about her. I'm going to see that you are made well."

The more Jagger wanted to argue the more his head pounded and the fog clouding his thoughts thickened. "What do I need to do to make myself better?"

"It's quite simple, young one. You must feed and you must unleash your vampire side. Tonight there will be bloodshed. And you have to do what comes natural to us. Feed."

"No innocents."

The older vampire chuckled. "No one is truly innocent, young one."

"But —"

"No buts. Listen to me ... I am your father, after all."

When their flight was underway, Sasha's nerves felt as though they would snap. Throughout the plane ride, not only was she worried about her son, she wondered what could have happened in Germany that resulted in this hasty visit.

Niccolo only gave her snippets of information even when she demanded that he tell her more. She thought he was probably trying to shield her from the truth, but keeping her in the dark was a sure way to drive her insane. It didn't help that despite the gravity of their circumstances, there was an undeniable sexual tension between them.

Sitting so close to him on the plane, hearing him breathe, smelling his cologne, and wanting to touch him was torture. She remembered their stolen night together and it made her want more. She tried to ignore it by feigning sleep, except after several minutes, she really did fall asleep.

*Sasha walked into Niccolo's room to find him packing. "You're leaving so soon?" she asked tentatively. She devoured his handsome face with her gaze. He was so beautiful it almost hurt to look at him. It almost seemed unfair for one man to be so appealing. From the moment she'd laid eyes on him, she loved him.*

*At six-foot-three, he was an entire foot taller than her. Though he was lean, he had broad shoulders, the kind that women wanted to rest their heads on. His wavy black hair was clipped short in the back, while thick dark locks rested casually on his forehead.*

*He had the face of an aristocrat with his high cheekbones and long, straight nose. His dark brows were thick, but arched attractively over his amber eyes. One smoldering look from him made her body quake with need. And his lips. Sasha had lost count of how many times she'd imagined them pressed all over her body.*

*Even the tiny gap between his two front teeth gave him a boyish charm when he smiled. She could find no fault in his countenance, but his looks weren't the only thing she found attractive about him. He was genuine, smart, and she often found herself smiling at his dry wit. She'd known from the beginning a man like him would be loyal to those he loved for all eternity. Her soul called out to his. He might not realize it, but they belonged together despite everything that had happened.*

*Niccolo answered without turning to face her. "I am hardly welcome here anymore, not that it matters. I have nothing to stay for now that Petra —" He stopped mid-sentence.*

*Sasha felt a lump rise in her throat. She still couldn't believe her beautiful sister was gone. Despite their differences, she'd cared about her sister. "I know my parents were harsh in blaming you for what happened, but don't take it to heart. They lost their daughter and when you hurt, you say things you don't mean."*

*"Is that so, strega?" He shrugged and continued to pack.*

She walked all the way into the room and closed the door.

"What do you want?" He still didn't turn around.

"I thought maybe you'd want to talk about your feelings with someone. I know how badly you must feel and I wanted to apologize for the way my parents treated you at the crossing over ceremony."

"What makes you think I would want to discuss how I feel with you? What's to discuss? She's gone. Now I begin to understand why your parents seemed so annoyed when you're around."

Sasha gasped. It was probably the grief talking, but he had never been rude to her before. "I'm sorry to have bothered you. My family is still taking care of some last minute formalities, but on their behalf, I wish you a safe journey home." As Sasha turned to leave, he was suddenly in front of her in the blink of an eye. He looked down at her with such a dark expression that she took a step back.

"Why aren't you with them? She was your sister."

Sasha laughed without humor. "I'm as unwelcome there as you are."

"So you came here to offer me comfort? What makes you think I would want to be comforted by a scrawny little strega like you?" He grabbed her by the elbows, looking down at her with glowing amber eyes.

"I know you're upset over Petra, but I've done nothing for you to treat me this way. I thought — "

"Yes, I know. You thought you could take Petra's place in my bed. How desperate are you to come to me now of all times?"

She shook her head vehemently. "I didn't come for that. I swear."

"So you're denying you've come to offer me a special kind of comfort? Don't think I haven't noticed the way you've watched me. I know you think you're in love with me, but I assure you, you are not."

"Don't tell me how I feel!" she protested, trying to free herself from his grasp, but his grip was too tight.

*"Fair enough, but I can certainly tell you how I feel. I resent that you've watched me and made me feel things I know I shouldn't. Although it is your sister I love, it is you whom I haven't been able to stop thinking about. You!" He cupped her face in his hands. "Dio, what is it about you? You're not even beautiful, but you've haunted my dreams. Damn you for making me feel this way!"*

*Before she realized what was happening, his mouth was on hers. She tried to pull away but his tongue slid between her parted lips. Sasha had been kissed before, but not quite like this.*

*The slow sensual way his tongue explored her mouth sent waves of rapture surging through her body. She felt like a flower opening up to the sun. Sasha had never before felt this way from just a kiss.*

*As he kissed her, his thumbs caressed the sides of her face. She moaned into his mouth. This is what she had dreamed of since the moment she had met Niccolo Grimaldi. She wrapped her arms around his neck, pressing her body against his. She had the urgent need to be closer to him. The hardness of his body against hers was so highly arousing.*

*"What am I doing?" he murmured against her mouth.*

*"Don't think, just feel," she whispered.*

*He muttered a curse before lifting her up in his arms and carrying her the short distance to the bed and dropping her onto it. She shivered as he practically ripped his clothes from his body impatiently, his eyes never leaving her. There was a feral gleam in the depths of his amber eyes that frightened and excited her at the same time.*

*When he stood completely naked, her breath caught in her throat. His body was just as magnificent as she had imagined it would be. He had a broad, well-toned chest, which tapered to a narrow waist and hips. His stomach was rippled with muscles and dark hair was liberally sprinkled across his chest. Still, the most magnificent part of him was his cock. It was so long, thick, and hard.*

*Sasha wanted to wrap her fingers around it and run her tongue over the tip, which was now a shade between pink and red. She licked her lips nervously.*

*"Do you like what you see, Sasha? Does my cock tempt you?"* Her throat went dry as he grasped his cock in his fist and slid his hand over his turgid length. It was so long and thick. Her eyes were riveted to the erotic sight of the slow back-and-forth motion. She never realized how much of a turn on it would be watch the man of her desire pleasure himself for her benefit. Sasha's tongue snaked out to lick her suddenly dry lips.

*"You like this, don't you?"*

She could only nod, not trusting herself to speak. How was it possible for one man to possess so much beauty? It just didn't seem fair.

*"Do you know how much you excite me? Heaven knows why I should want you so, but I do. I want to see your body now. Take off your clothes. My cock is in need of your sweet pussy."*

Sasha scrambled off the bed and started to undo the buttons on her blouse. Her fingers seemed suddenly clumsy.

*"Dio! You'll take all night!"* He swiftly removed her clothes, demonstrating his obvious familiarity with undressing women. The thought of him with other women caused her to feel an irrational wave of jealousy, but she quickly suppressed it. She was the one in his arms now, and this was the way things were supposed to be. Within a matter of seconds, she was nude.

Niccolo stared at her with a hungry expression in his glowing eyes. She realized she was about to become his main course. *"You've been holding out on me, strega. You have a beautiful body."*

She could feel herself blushing. No one had ever told her that before, but then again, she had never been intimate with a man before. She was glad that he would be her first.

*"Your breasts are small but perfect; they will fit in my mouth just fine,"* he said, before bending his head to run his tongue over one swollen nipple.

She moaned, grabbing his shoulders to keep her balance. The swirl of his tongue on her sensitive peak made her cry out in pleasure. *The feel of his mouth sent bursts of sensation from her head to her toes.* "Oh, Niccolo, that feels so good."

In response, he increased the pressure of his mouth on her breast. Her pussy clenched with need, and Sasha could feel her thighs dampening. She never wanted the deliciousness of this moment to end.

Niccolo lifted his head briefly to transfer his attention to her other breast. He nibbled on her nipple, sending pulses of pleasure to her pussy. She was so hot for him that she could barely think. He squeezed and kneaded her breasts as he played with her nipples.

When she felt his incisors sink into her breast, she cried out in surprise. It was just a little prick that didn't really hurt at all. She knew enough about vampires to know that the sharing of blood during lovemaking was a very sensual and intimate act. That he wanted to feed from her thrilled her beyond anything she could ever imagine. This had to mean he felt something for her as well, something beyond lust. They would be together forever after this, she thought happily.

He must have sucked on her breast for several minutes before lifting his head. He had already retracted his incisors.

"I can smell your pussy. You're wet and ready for me, aren't you?" He grinned before licking away drop of dark ruby blood from the corner of his mouth.

"Yes. Please make love to me," she begged.

"This isn't making love, this is fucking."

Before Sasha could reply Niccolo's mouth covered hers once more. She could taste the coppery sweetness of her blood on his tongue mixed with the unique flavor of Niccolo. She became delirious with desire. He pushed her back to the bed. "I want to eat your pussy badly, but my cock hurts. I need to fuck, now."

Sasha gasped at his sudden roughness. He pulled her thighs apart and without hesitation, plunged into her pussy.

"Oh, God!" Despite his size and her smallness, she'd known there would be some pain, but it wasn't unbearable. Nothing would make her push him away; to remain close to him, she would have endured an eternity of pain.

" Por Dio! *Why didn't you tell me you're a virgin?"*

*The initial pain of his entry slowly subsided, but the sheer size of his cock within her untried pussy was still somewhat uncomfortable.* "Does it matter? This is what we both wanted. Just give me a moment to adjust."

"How could you have lived for nearly seventy years without a man?" *he asked incredulously.*

*There was no way she'd tell him that she had been holding out for someone she was in love with. Sasha didn't think he was ready to hear how she felt about him just yet.*

*"It's doesn't matter. Please don't stop."*

*"You must believe I'm an animal if you think I want to hurt you like this."*

*She could tell he was trying to be gallant even as his cock pulsed inside of her. She knew he wanted to move in and out of her.*

*"The pain has gone away. Please. Do what you want with me." She lifted her hips up.*

*They both gasped as he sank deeper into her. The pain had indeed faded into a dull ache, but the feeling of being one with the man she loved was doing things to her senses. She needed him to finish or she would go crazy.*

*"Please, Niccolo."*

*"Damn, I must be insane," he muttered before he grasped her thighs and began to thrust within her. At first it was very uncomfortable, but as his cock speared back and forth she felt lust build up once more in the pit of her stomach.*

*A wave of passion flowed through her and she couldn't imagine how she could have lived before this moment.*

*"Your pussy is so damn tight and wet," he said, looking down at her with lust-filled amber eyes. She reached up to run her fingers*

over the well-defined muscles in his chest, reveling in the feel of his skin beneath her fingertips.

She wanted more, needed to be closer to him. "Kiss me." Sasha pulled him down.

The heat of his breath mingling with hers only served to inflame her more. He kissed her with a savagery that threatened to take her to the edge of insanity. She bucked her hips against him, meeting him thrust for delectable thrust. Sasha was on fire for this man.

She ripped her mouth away from his to scream out his name. "Oh, Niccolo!"

He increased his pace, plunging deeper and deeper into her with each thrust. She knew she would be sore afterward, but she didn't care. She needed this more than she needed air. Suddenly she felt an explosion in her so powerful and pleasurable that her body shook uncontrollably as she reached her peak.

Niccolo gripped her thighs again as he reared back onto his knees. With one last powerful thrust, he cried out. "Sasha, what have you done to me?"

He shuddered as he released his seed inside of her. Sasha squeezed her pussy muscles around his cock, milking it of every drop of his cum. Niccolo collapsed on top of her and she wrapped her arms around him. This was the moment she had been waiting for all her life.

She stroked a damp lock of his black hair as his heart beat against hers. "Mmm, that was everything I dreamed it would be." She smiled in content.

He stiffened. "This was a mistake." Niccolo abruptly pushed off of her and rolled to the edge of the bed. The look of disgust on his face made her heart plummet.

"A mistake? You enjoyed it as much as I did."

He slid off the bed and grabbed his discarded clothing. "That isn't the point. What we did was wrong."

*She sat up, silently praying for him to take back the words he'd just uttered. "How can it be wrong when this is meant to be?"*

*"I think not. What was meant to be was Petra and me. Just because she's gone doesn't mean I'm looking to fill a vacancy. And even if I were, you'd be the last person I'd choose. I must have been out of my mind. What have you done to me, dammit?"*

*Sasha gripped the sheets tightly around her body. His words flayed her like a whip, causing a great deal of pain. Despite this, she had to make him see what they'd shared was special. "I've done nothing to you. You're simply too stubborn to admit you feel something for me too. We both wanted this." She climbed out of bed as tears she didn't bother to wipe away slid down her face.*

*Niccolo turned away from her as he dressed. She released the sheet, slipped off the bed and walked to him, naked and unashamed. When she touched him, he flinched. "Don't touch me. I don't know what you thought you'd accomplish with this seduction game of yours, but I want you to get out of my sight."*

*In that moment her world was caving in on her and Sasha didn't know how to stop it. "You can't mean this. What we shared was special."*

*He looked at her then with glowing eyes. "Get out of here now! The sooner I'm away from you and your family the better."*

*"But I love you," she whispered. Her plea was pathetic, but she had no shame where Niccolo was involved.*

*"That's unfortunate because I don't love you." She stepped back at the harshness of his tone. "Don't ever speak of love to me again. I could never love you. You are not half the woman your sister was. Now leave me."*

*If he would have ripped her heart out and stamped on it several times, it would have hurt less. She picked up her clothes and hurried to the door. Before she left, she faced him one last time. "One of the reasons I love you is because I sensed your beautiful soul. Now I know I was wrong. You have no soul." She ran out of the room.*

"Sasha, wake up."

She jolted awake to find herself back on the plane. It took her several moments to gather her thoughts. Niccolo looked at her with a brooding expression.

Damn. She had been dreaming. It was the same dream she had every night since their one and only time together. "Are we here?" she asked, still drowsy.

"The plane will land in a few minutes. Someone will be waiting for us at the gate."

She nodded as she glanced away. Sasha wondered how she would make it through this ordeal, because despite all that had happened and the time that had passed, she still loved him.

## Chapter Six

When their flight landed at Munich Airport, Niccolo could not remember ever feeling more relieved in his life. The plane ride had been excruciating with Sasha sitting so close to him. They had barely spoken throughout the long, arduous trip, and that was just fine with him. Unfortunately, when she had dozed off, her head had fallen onto his shoulder.

His first instinct had been to push her away, but the scent of her shampoo had wafted to his nostrils—honeysuckle and jasmine. With her dark lashes resting against her pale skin, she had looked so pretty and angelic in her sleep that Niccolo had been tempted to kiss her. He had to know if she tasted as good as he remembered or if he had built up their one time together to be more than it actually had been.

His dick had been hard for the majority of the trip. Damn the witch! It was obvious to him that she still held some kind of thrall over him. Why else would his thoughts be consumed of nothing else but her being naked beneath him when his main concern should be the whereabouts of his son? The discomfort of his arousal for the duration of the trip had put in a decidedly foul mood, and it was all Sasha's fault.

As soon as the passengers were cleared to leave, he gripped her forearm none too gently. "Let's go. A car should be waiting for us," he said gruffly.

As she stood, she snatched her arm away. "I can manage without you manhandling me."

Niccolo shot her a glare as he waited impatiently for the other passengers to go by. It was a pain in the ass to fly commercial, but it was more inconspicuous and threw off any enemies who might be on their tail. When the aisle was clear, he grabbed Sasha's hand and pulled her along with him. He strode through the airport with purposeful strides.

"Slow down. I can barely keep up with you," she said from behind him.

He sighed and slowed down to accommodate her shorter legs.

"Sasha!" a voice called from behind them.

*What now?*

Niccolo turned to see who had called out to her. His eyes narrowed when he saw the look of pleasure that crossed Sasha's face.

"Yuri!" Snatching her hand from his grasp, Sasha ran to the tall blond man. Niccolo knew right away that the man was not human or a vampire. The stranger lifted her into his arms and swung her around as though they were a couple of children. A sudden burst of anger rushed through him. He realized that he had no right to feel this way, but who the hell did this man think he was to hold her like that?

He was tall, yet still a couple of inches shorter than Niccolo. He had no clue who this Yuri character was in relation to Sasha, but he didn't appreciate the way the other man looked at her.

"Sasha, you look more beautiful every time I see you. What are you doing here in Munich?" Yuri smoothed her hair back in an intimate gesture, and Niccolo wanted to break his goddamn fingers.

"I—"

Niccolo approached them before Sasha could answer. "She's with me, and we're looking for *our* son, so, as touching as this little reunion is, we really must go." He gripped Sasha's arm, his gaze never leaving Yuri's face. There was something about him Niccolo didn't like, but he didn't have time to analyze it.

"Nikita is missing?" Yuri ignored Niccolo and looked down at Sasha. Nikita? Who was this interloper and how close was he to Jagger that he called him Nikita?

"Yes, my son is missing and I'm frightened that something has happened to him."

"He's no longer a boy, but a man. He's most likely okay," Yuri suggested.

"A mother knows."

"*Moy angelochek.* You worry too much." Yuri brushed Sasha's cheek with the back of his hand and Niccolo's blood began to boil.

"Sasha, let's go," he repeated between clenched teeth, trying to rein in his temper.

Yuri finally turned his dark gaze to Niccolo, a hint of challenge in his eyes. "So you are Nikita's father." It was a statement not a question.

"And you are?" Niccolo raised a brow.

"Yuri Khrushchev. I'm a friend of the Romanovs and a *very close personal friend* of Sasha's."

Niccolo didn't miss the fact that Yuri had emphasized the words "very close" and "personal friend." The asshole obviously didn't know he was two seconds away from getting his heart ripped out. "Good for you. Sasha, we need to go. Now!" he growled.

She looked back and forth at both men with uncertainty on her face. "Yuri, Niccolo is right. We must go. I'm sorry we couldn't have met under better circumstances."

She turned to go, but Yuri grabbed her shoulder. *"Ya pomoguo tebe."* Yuri spoke to Sasha in Russian as though Niccolo were some dolt who wouldn't understand.

This time he would not excuse the man's rudeness. "We don't need your help, thank you very much. I suggest you release her or you will feel my fist in your face."

"Do not make threats, vampire. You'll find that I am not one to be trifled with."

"Oh? I—"

"Stop it! Both of you are behaving like a couple of ridiculous children. Jagger is missing and he is what's important here. Niccolo, Yuri is my friend and he wants to help us look for our son. What is the harm of one more person searching for him? Yuri has many skills which could prove very helpful." She faced the other man and looked at him pleadingly. "Yuri, I would appreciate your help, but Niccolo isn't used to your sense of humor. He doesn't understand that you were only joking."

Niccolo knew damn well Yuri had meant what he had said.

"I'm sorry, Sasha. I didn't mean to upset you, but you must allow me to aide in your search." Yuri smiled at her.

"Of course," she readily agreed, "but why are you at the airport? I wouldn't want you to derail your plans."

Yuri smiled. "I was going to take a pleasure trip. I can go anytime. It's not as important as searching for Nikita."

"Well, if you're sure. I'd love your help."

"No." Niccolo contradicted.

"He's my son, too, Niccolo, and I say Yuri comes with us."

He was seething. The little control he was holding onto was quickly slipping away.

"Yes, Grimaldi, don't be petty. Besides, I've been more of a father to Nikita than you have."

Niccolo's slammed his fist into Yuri's face.

Yuri went reeling back as an onlooker screamed.

"How could you?" Sasha looked at Niccolo as if were the one in the wrong.

Yuri slowly made it to his feet. "You will pay for this, vampire."

Niccolo noticed that the palms of Yuri's hands were glowing. A warlock. He should have known.

"I do hope you two aren't about to fight because I'll be very pissed that I wasn't invited." Romeo spoke from behind them. "Now, may I suggest that we all get the hell out of here and settle this away from prying eyes?"

There were too many people watching them and he knew any minute that airport security would be on their tail. Niccolo took Sasha's arm and they left the terminal.

A limo was waiting for them when they got outside. As they were about to get into the vehicle, Niccolo turned to Sasha's friend. "You're not coming with us."

"You can't tell me what I can and can't do. Besides, Sasha wants me with her, don't you?" Yuri asked her.

She nodded. "Yes. Please. The more people we have looking for him, the sooner we will find him. Your skills will come in handy."

Yuri shot Niccolo a smug look of triumph.

Niccolo clenched his fists.

*Easy, Nico, he's trying to provoke you. Don't let him get to you,* Romeo's voice entered his mind.

*Since when have you ever backed down from a fight?* Niccolo shot back.

*I would kick his scrawny ass myself if there was time, but Dante needs to see us right away. Things don't look good, Nico. There's been another slaughter today – just like the first.*

Niccolo's heart seized up. What had his son become involved in? He let out a mental sigh. *You are right, but if that bastard makes one more offhand comment, I will shove my fist down his thrown and pull out his fucking spine.*

*If that bastard says anything to upset you, I won't stop you.* Romeo winked at him and they all got into the limo.

Yuri held Sasha's hand as they rode to the house where Dante and his Underground agents were gathered. She couldn't believe the scene Niccolo had made. He almost acted as if he was jealous, but it couldn't be because of her. It had to be because Yuri had been in Jagger's life when Niccolo hadn't been. Yuri's comment had been uncalled for, too, and she intended to bring it up to him in private.

She could feel Niccolo's gaze on her and she tried not to meet the intensity of his amber stare The way he stared at her if it was almost as if he was looking right into her soul. If he read her mind now, he would know the truth of her feelings for him, and that was the last thing she wanted. She took comfort in the fact that the likelihood of him penetrating her thoughts was slim; most immortals could shield their thoughts, so Niccolo probably believed he couldn't read her mind.

She peeked at Niccolo through her lashes. She was still in awe over this gorgeous man but she hoped it didn't show. Much. Over the years, she had tried to stop loving him, but everyone she had dated since him had lacked something. She'd come close to being intimate with a few men, but something always stopped her at the last minute. Sasha was sure it was the memory of Niccolo.

*I'm a fool.*

She wished she could hate him for the way he had callously discarded her after they'd made love. Niccolo Grimaldi wasn't an easy man to forget, especially when their son was the spitting image of him. She doubted she'd ever stop loving him. And yet, he was incapable of returning that love until the enchantment spell was broken. At least that's why she told herself. Even without the spell, there was a slim chance that he might not love her then, either.

She stole one more glance at him and her heart skipped a beat. He and his brother were silent, but she could tell they were communicating telepathically.

"What's on your mind, *milaya moya?*" Yuri leaned over to whisper in her ear.

She focused her attention on Yuri, whose presence she had almost forgotten. He was an old friend of her family and had provided her with a lot of emotional support through the years, taking her out when she needed a pick-me-up, and making her feel good about herself when she was sad. Although Yuri was like another uncle to Jagger and one of her best friends, he made no secret of his desire to be more than friends with her. Sasha, however, didn't want to ruin their friendship. She appreciated the fact that he seemed to accept that.

She sighed. "I'm thinking about my son. I'm worried."

"He'll be okay."

"How can you be so sure?" She wanted more than anything to believe him.

"I just know. *Pover'te mne.*"

She didn't respond. Despite his words, how could she trust him in this when her gut told her Jagger was in trouble? It was very inconvenient to not be able to use her powers when they were needed the most. *Damn you, Papa!*

Yuri grasped her chin and turned her head so that their gazes locked. "I wish I could take that sad look from your eyes."

"Thank you, Yuri, but the only thing that will make me feel better is seeing Jagger and making sure he's okay."

"I understand, but until then I have a shoulder for you to lean on."

He put his arm around her and she rested her head against his chest. She closed her eyes, surrendering to the comfort he offered. If only he were Niccolo.

It was crazy for her to hold on to the hope he'd ever see her in that light when he'd made it quite plain he never would. But she had to keep telling herself it was because of the spell. She hoped he'd soon see things for the way they are, because each time he glared at her or spoke to her as if her feelings didn't matter, a little bit of her died inside.

The occupants of the limo were silent as it tore down the road, taking them to their destination. Finally, she felt the car come to a halt, and she lifted her head. When she opened her eyes, she found herself staring into an angry pair of amber eyes. What was he so upset about now?

"If you are finished cuddling with your boyfriend, perhaps you'd like to get out of the car so we can find out where our son might be." Niccolo said the words with such hostility she was rendered speechless.

Actually, she was getting tired of this shit. He hadn't said a word to her during the entire trip, and now he was acting this way? She didn't bother to respond.

Everyone got out of the limo while she took in the grand house. She turned to Romeo, not even bothering to look at the dark-haired vampire who was still glaring at her. "Where are we?"

"This is my friend Wolf's home. Everyone else is already inside. Knowing Dante, he's probably wondering what the hell is taking us so long." Romeo headed for the door.

"Come on, Sasha." Yuri held out his hand. She was about to take it when Niccolo grabbed her arm.

"Sasha and I need to talk. Why don't you go inside, Khrushchev?"

Yuri seemed as if he wanted to protest but Sasha shook her head to tell him to stand down. He smiled at her. "Give me a shout if you need me," he said instead and bent down to kiss her cheek. He shot Niccolo an insolent glare before following Romeo inside the house.

Sasha knew whatever Niccolo wanted to say, she wasn't going to like it, so she tried to put him off. "We should go in, too. The others are waiting for us."

"Who is Khrushchev to you?" he demanded.

He had to be kidding. She didn't have time for this shit. Sasha attempted to walk past him but he caught her wrist. "Let me go. I'm tired of you grabbing me like you have that right."

"Who the fuck is he to you?" His incisors descended in his anger and his eyes glowed.

If she weren't so angry herself she'd be frightened, but she was tired of him treating her like dirt one second and then pretending like he actually cared the next. "None of your damn business! How dare you demand answers from me like it is your place?"

"You are the mother of my son and if this man has been in Jagger's life, I want to know. Are you lovers?"

She was tempted to slap him but knew it would further incite him. "You may be entitled to know about the goings-on in Jagger's life, but not in mine. You forfeited that right years ago. Now, I'm going inside." She attempted to maneuver around him when he suddenly hauled her up against him and his mouth swooped down on hers.

Sasha was too surprised to protest or respond as he kissed her with an angry hunger. His sharp incisors grazed her lips but she kept them firmly closed.

"Open your mouth, dammit," he muttered against her mouth.

When she didn't comply, he tugged her hair roughly, making her cry out. Niccolo's tongue darted forward and damned if she didn't feel a warmth in the pit of her stomach. That all-too-familiar tingling sensation began to spiral through her body.

Just as quickly as he'd grabbed her, Niccolo pushed her away. "*Strega!* Release me! Years ago you accused your sister of casting a spell, but it was you, wasn't it?" He shook her.

"I didn't! I wouldn't do such a thing."

"Liar! You did. Why else does my cock grow hard at the mere thought of you? Why do I lay awake at night wanting you? Why do I want you so much even though our son is missing? Release me instantly, witch!"

"I can't release you because I never put a spell on you, Niccolo. I respected you too much to do something like that to you. Besides, I can't put a spell on anyone even if I could."

His eyes narrowed. "What the hell is that supposed to mean?"

"My father has bound my powers. I haven't been able to use my abilities since the night of Petra's death."

Niccolo seemed so stunned by her admission he released her. Sasha used that opportunity to make it past him and into the house. Now her humiliation was complete.

## Chapter Seven

Niccolo was still in a state of shock when he made it into the house. If what Sasha said was true and her powers really were bound, then everything he thought about her was wrong. All these years he had been living in a cloud. Were things even the way he recalled? Why had her father taken her powers?

It made no sense. If she'd lost her abilities then why did it feel like he was being held in her thrall? How could he explain the uncontrollable lust he felt whenever she was near that drove him to distraction? It made him question what he had felt for Petra.

"It's good to see you've finally joined us, Nico," Dante welcomed him with a crooked smile and a raised black brow.

"Sorry," Niccolo muttered, his mind still reeling from Sasha's revelation.

The comfortable sitting room was full of people, including Romeo and Dante in the center. Their host Wolf, nodded in acknowledgement to Niccolo before returning his attention to Dante. Two of Dante's lieutenants sat on the far end of the room. Angel Ramirez and Carter McKenna had been in the Underground for several years and were two of Dante's most trusted agents. Niccolo liked both vampires, but it was hard to trust anyone, especially after the Trent Black affair —a betrayal and murder they had yet to solve.

Niccolo's gaze drifted to Sasha. She looked paler than normal and her dark eyes looked larger than ever in her small face. She sat on the couch with Yuri's arm draped possessively over her shoulder. Niccolo's jaw clenched. When this was all over and he was assured of his son's safety, he planned on beating the shit out of Khrushchev.

*Are you okay?* Romeo's voice entered his mind.

*We'll talk about it later.*

*Is it Khrushchev? I'm not averse to fucking him up. There's something about him that I don't like or trust.*

*I know. You said so in the limo, but let's first hear what Dante has to say about Jagger before we rip this asshole to shreds."*

Romeo nodded. *Naturally, but if he makes a single move that I don't like, he's dust.*

*Of course,* Niccolo agreed before closing off his mind. He turned his attention to Dante. "Tell us what this is all about. How is my son involved?"

"I'm not really sure what his exact involvement is. We're still in the discovery phase of this mission. As I told you over the phone, I picked up a scent a lot like yours, but I knew you were still in L.A.," Dante said. "I felt an overwhelming connection with the vampires who had been there."

"What happened?" Niccolo wanted to know.

"There was a function—some kind of party with about twenty or so people. Someone crashed the event and left no survivors. It definitely looked like the work of rogues, but we all know that rogues generally don't bother humans, and if they do, they don't leave messes of this magnitude. They certainly never leave bodies behind. It seems someone is trying to send a message, but we don't know who, why, or what. Not long before you arrived, we got word that there was another incident just like it between here and the Austrian border."

Dante looked troubled by the news, although he had seen a lot of carnage in his lifetime. Niccolo knew then that there was something Dante wasn't revealing. He was about to challenge him about it, but Carter stood up.

"It was very similar to the first killings. There was lots of blood smeared on the walls, and it looked like a feeding had taken place. The media is reporting these incidents as some kind of satanic ritual murders. From what I could see, rogues were not the only immortals involved in this slaughter — there were shifters. Some of the claw and bite marks were very distinctive."

"Rogues and shifters? Rogues usually work alone, and shifters only hunt with their own pack members, at least for the most part," Niccolo mused out loud.

"Judging from the scene, that's the only logical conclusion we could come up with," Carter added.

"Jagger cannot possibly be involved in this. You must be mistaken about picking up his scent." Niccolo knew he was grasping at straws. Dante was rarely wrong when it came to their work.

"Do you think I want this to be true, Nico?" Dante shot at him.

Before Niccolo could respond, Sasha sprang to her feet. "I don't care what you want. My son wouldn't have done that! You're wrong!"

"I hope to God that I am, Sasha. I can appreciate your anxiety at the moment. I'm just as concerned about my nephew's safety as you, but we have to keep cool heads or nothing will be accomplished." Dante walked over to her and put his hand on her shoulder in a comforting gesture.

She shrugged his hand off. "You tell me to be calm, but it is easier said than done. And I doubt anyone can care as much about his well-being than his mother. Jagger ... he's all I have in this world. If anything bad were to happen to him..." Her voice trailed off, and she looked on the verge of tears, with Niccolo aching for her because he understood her pain.

Dante tried to reassure her. "I promise you that we'll do everything in our power to find him."

"I just want to make sure he's safe. I know he's a man, but he's still my baby. If only ... Oh, God," she held her face in her hands and began to sob loudly.

"You see what you've done, Grimaldi? You've upset her. Why are you standing around here just talking about it? Perhaps you don't care about Nikita as much as you say you do." Yuri stood up, stalked over to Sasha and pulled her into his arms.

Niccolo clenched his fists at his side, because he sorely wanted to slam them it into the insolent warlock's face.

Dante glared at Khrushchev. "I'm sure you think you have a purpose for being here, though you weren't invited —"

"Sasha wants me here," the warlock declared defiantly.

"Then if you want to stay here, I'd suggest you be careful with what you say. Whether you're wanted here or not, keep your mouth shut and stop making a bad situation worse," Dante advised.

Niccolo saw Romeo take a step toward Khrushchev, but Niccolo shook his head.

The warlock seemed unfazed by the animosity simmering in the room. An amused gleam entered his eyes. "So this is how the Grimaldis operate—by ganging up on one man. I suppose all the talk of your greatness has been just that—talk."

Sasha looked up at her friend with clear disbelief in her dark eyes. She shook her head and pushed away from him. "Yuri, what's gotten into you? Your comments are quite unnecessary."

"Yes, listen to her, Khrushchev. You're walking a very fine line tonight. Don't give me a reason to rip your sorry ass apart right here and now," Niccolo spoke with the little bit of control he had left.

"A threat? How predictable." The warlock laughed, but was cut off abruptly when Niccolo gripped him by the throat.

Niccolo had had enough of Khrushchev's asinine taunts. He couldn't remember another time when he had let someone get under his skin this much. His incisors descended and his fingers shifted, the long nails digging into the warlock's neck.

"Niccolo!" Sasha cried out with horror, but he ignored her.

Khrushchev attempted to pry the vampire's fingers from around his neck, but Niccolo held on tightly. The warlock's face went from a bright red to a purplish hue.

Dante tried to pry them apart, but Niccolo's rage made it hard for him to budge his younger brother. Romeo and Wolf joined Dante in his efforts to release the warlock.

"That's enough!" Sasha voice drifted to his ears but didn't completely register. Eventually, her voice broke through, and he loosened his hold around Khrushchev's throat.

The warlock pulled away gasping and coughing for air. "You ... will ... pay ... for ... this ... Grimaldi." A bright bolt of what looked like lightning shot from Yuri's palm and struck Niccolo in the chest. Niccolo was knocked of his feet by the energy burst and flew across the room. He landed on his ass, but he was back on his feet immediately and rushed toward his adversary.

Dante and Romeo grabbed him before he could reach Khrushchev. Niccolo struggled to break free of the hands restraining him.

"You do that again and I will strangle you myself," Dante warned the warlock.

"Am I not allowed to defend myself?" Yuri questioned defiantly as he rubbed his bruised neck. "Your brother needs to learn to control himself."

Dante's eyes flashed. "He didn't do anything the rest of us would not have done when similarly provoked. Anyway, I warmed you about keeping your comments to yourself. I don't care who wants you here, because it's time for you to leave."

"And if I don't?" the warlock challenged.

"Then I'll release my brother."

Romeo grinned. "I actually wouldn't mind seeing what will happen if we let Nico go. How about it, Dante?"

"Shut up, Ro."

Romeo chuckled, seeming to take no offense. "Spoilsport."

"He's here because I want him to be. He's my friend and he's as anxious to find Jagger as I am. Instead of fighting, can't we try a truce for my son's sake?" Sasha pleaded. "I promise he'll keep his opinions to himself from now on."

Sasha's words made sense, but Niccolo wasn't in the mood to be rational, especially since her hand now rested protectively against the warlock's chest. He nearly burst a blood vessel he was so pissed.

Wolf stepped forward. "Look, everyone, tensions are running high and we all need to think about what our priorities are here. One, Jagger is missing, and two, rogues are slaughtering innocent people. Considering tonight's events, we can be certain that these killings will happen again. Remember what we're here for and leave the hard feelings at the door. When this is all settled, you two can rip each other apart, but for now let's focus on finding Jagger."

Niccolo flushed. Wolf was right. His son was missing and he was trying to brawl. Shit. "All right, you guys can let go now. Let's formulate a plan."

Khrushchev glared at him. Let the bastard glare all he wanted; there was no way he would allow the warlock to rile him again ... at least not until things were settled.

Dante released him with obvious reluctance. He walked to the center of the room, taking charge once again. "Sasha, Wolf, thank you for being the voices of reason. Now, back to business. I think the best thing to do is to split up in teams. Romeo and Wolf, I want you to go back to where the first massacre occurred and gather any more information you can. There shouldn't be as much activity there now as there was earlier. Glamour anyone who speculates beyond more than what is being reported by the media. The last thing we need are people questioning our existence. Carter, you'll come with me to investigate the second site. Nico and Angel, I'll need you to head toward Vienna. Given the two previous locations, they're probably headed south."

Sasha clutched Dante's arm. "What about me? I can't just sit here and do nothing. I need to help."

"You will be a big help by staying here. We need someone to stay put to be our central communication coordinator. I have other agents working on leads elsewhere, and should one of them stop by, it would be helpful to have someone here." Dante patted her shoulder briefly.

"Don't worry, I'll be here with you." Khrushchev took Sasha's hand and pulled her against him.

Niccolo grinded his teeth in frustration. The ugly head of jealousy reared and he hated feeling this way about a woman whom he was supposed to have no feelings for. He couldn't wait until this ordeal was over because he planned to work her out of his system once and for all. And if that included fucking her until he was finally sated, then so be it.

<><><><><>

Sasha watched helplessly as the vampires departed. *Damn them all!* She refused to be some useless damsel in distress. If they thought she would sit idly by while they went out on their search, they had another think coming. "We need leave and do our own investigation. Perhaps you could involve a search spell."

"You know I would need a personal item from Nikita to invoke such a spell. Besides, if we go look for him where would we even start? Let the vampires search; they can use their skills to track Nikita down more effectively."

She frowned at the casualness of his tone. "I'm not staying here. How can you be so calm about this? I thought you loved Jagger."

"I do. I love him as though he was mine, and I am hurt that you would doubt me. And I love you too. The fact that I'm still here after that beast attacked me should be proof of that." Yuri sounded indignant. "I cannot believe he tried to kill me."

Sasha couldn't believe it, either. She didn't quite understand what had come over Niccolo. She had always thought him a calm, steady man, but tonight she saw a side of him that frightened her. He acted as if he was jealous, but he had made it clear time and time again that he didn't care about her. Maybe it was simply that Niccolo and Yuri rubbed each other the wrong way.

"Yuri, I'm not going to try to justify what Niccolo did. He should never have gotten physical with you, but you were out of line for saying those things to him. What were you thinking?"

"I don't like him."

"That still doesn't justify you acting like an asshole. You're not normally like this. In case you have forgotten, he's Jagger's father, and I would be grateful it if you don't speak like that to him again."

"How can you defend that bastard after what he's done to you?"

"You don't know the situation. Don't assume that you do."

He gripped her shoulders, forcing her to meet his gaze. "Sasha, can't you see I'm concerned for you? Do you know what it's like for me to watch you pine away for someone so unworthy of your love when I've loved you for so long? I would be much better for you than he."

She shook loose from his hold and turned her back to him. She wasn't ready to discuss this now. Sasha already had told him that she could never love him other than as a friend. "You are aware of how I feel, Yuri. I thought you respected that."

"It's very hard to not express my feelings. Don't condemn me because I love you." Yuri grabbed her by the forearm and turned her around to face him once more. There was pain in his dark eyes, and it made her sad. The last thing she wanted to do was to hurt him, but it wouldn't have been fair to pretend a love she didn't feel.

"I'm sorry. I'll understand if you don't want to help me now, but whether it means anything to you or not, I do care about you and I don't want you to get hurt by Niccolo or his brothers. They're all very old and powerful; if you cross them, they will crush you."

Yuri flared his nostrils and sneered. "I'm not scared of them. Your precious Niccolo and his damn brothers are too arrogant for their own good. They even have you believing the hype. Mark my words, Sasha. They'll all soon get their comeuppance. Change is coming and the Grimaldis had better watch out." The animosity radiating from him made her take away from him.

"What are you saying, Yuri? You're not making any sense."

"It will all make sense in time."

Sasha suspected he was holding something back but decided to drop it—for the moment. There would be time to figure out what he meant after she found her son. In the meantime, she was wasting precious time standing around. "I'm leaving, whether I have your assistance or not."

"I don't think—

"There's nothing to think about. Will you come with me or do I go this alone?"

He moved closer and grazed her cheek with his fingertips. "I'd never leave you in your time of need."

"Thank you, Yuri." She headed for the door but she didn't look back. For the first time, ever, she didn't feel comfortable being around her friend.

## Chapter Eight

"*Madre de Dios!* I have never seen anything like this." Angel exclaimed in shock as they entered a building just outside of Vienna.

"Nor have I." Niccolo shuddered at the sight. Though he wasn't particularly religious, he made the sign of the cross in the air. The small office in which they stood was suitable for maybe thirty or so people. Niccolo tried to wrap his head around the sheer carnage of the scene. In over six hundred years he had never seen such bloodshed. Bodies lay on the ground, limbs were ripped off, and a putrid smell filled the air. All the victims were human.

Niccolo's breath caught in his throat. A woman lay naked on a desk, her head dangling at an odd angle. When he touched the head, it fell off. He jumped back. "The bastards!"

Angel knelt down beside the body of a mutilated man who didn't look much older than Jagger. "This was very recent. The blood is still warm." Angel stood up, wiping the blood he had touched onto the side of his pants. "We've not missed the perpetrators by much. We may still be able to catch up with them."

Niccolo sighed in frustration. He had learned quite a few things by studying this scene. Rogues were indeed responsible for this, as well as shifters. Something else bothered him, however. Why had no one had heard these people scream? Other forces must be working here. Witches? Warlocks? Jagger? "No. I think there may be other factors involved; they'll be long gone by now."

A new scent wafted to his nose. It was familiar, yet foreign, reminding him of when his brothers were near, but not quite. The smell was family. Jagger.

The very thought that his son could be involved in this frightened him to his very core. He hoped to God there was some logical explanation for this but the probability of it being something else wasn't good.

He realized then that despite all he had done to try and make Jagger's life easier, he still had not done enough. If his son were indeed involved, he placed the blame squarely at his own feet.

"Something is troubling you, my friend." Angel walked over to him.

"I can't imagine what must have been gone through these people's minds when it happened. Do you get the impression there are other powers involved — not just rogues, I mean."

"Yes. I got that too, but that's not what you're thinking about, is it?" Angel was too perceptive for his own good. "I sense a heaviness in your heart. It's your son, isn't it? Or perhaps the young witch you left back in Munich?"

Angel had been an agent with the Underground for nearly a century. Originally from Havana, he'd chosen to make his home base in the Dominican Republic where he owned several businesses. Angel had joined the Underground after rogues killed his sister. Although he was just over two hundred years old, his quick mind and analytical brain made him a very valuable member for the cause.

It also helped that he was attractive — at least the ladies seemed to think so — and oozed charm. Angel used his wit and looks to obtain lots of information which had been useful to the Underground over the years. However, he could be quite vicious when crossed. Aside from being a great asset, he'd also proven to be a good friend.

"Is it that obvious?" Niccolo asked.

"Well, I can only imagine how you must feel about your son's possible involvement, but the warlock back at Wolf's really upset you."

"He's got a big mouth."

"But it wasn't what he said, was it? I think you were more upset by how close he seems to be to your Sasha."

"She's not my Sasha! She's nothing to me except the mother of my son."

"Yet you could barely keep your eyes off her. I'm not as old as you are, but I can recognize that she is your bloodmate. What I can't figure out is why you're trying so hard to fight it."

"Angel, I think it's time for you to drop the subject. You don't know what you're talking about."

"You may not think so, but I have eyes."

"Dammit, you're just as infuriating as my brothers."

Angel chuckled. "It's an honor that you think so."

Niccolo turned away from the other vampire. He was more confused than ever. Sasha was *not* his bloodmate. How could she be when he felt so conflicted around her? His heart had belonged to Petra. Sasha was merely an inconvenience. His body was engaged where she was concerned, but his mind wasn't. He was about to tell Angel as much when a sudden movement caught his eye. From nowhere, a vampire appeared, claws out, teeth bared.

Niccolo and Angel went into battle mode. As the vampire approached, Niccolo dodged a blow aimed at him and slammed his palm into his attacker's chest. The assailant went flying back into the far wall.

Angel swiftly grabbed the vampire by the collar and slammed him into the wall again. To Niccolo's surprise, the vampire stopped fighting back, a defeated look in his eyes.

"Angel, stop," he commanded, when his friend was about to thrust the vampire into the wall again.

Angel hesitated for a moment before letting go.

"Kill me now and be done with it, rogues," the vampire muttered, his brown eyes flashing with defiance, blood dripping from the corner of his mouth.

Rogues? What was he talking about? "You're the one who attacked us," Niccolo pointed out as he drew closer to the vampire. Something was off kilter here. "What is your name?"

"My name isn't important, rogue. Just kill me and be done with it," the young vampire repeated.

"We had no plans to kill anyone, but I would suggest you cooperate before we change our minds."

"Liars! You two slaughtered all of these people."

"What the hell are you talking about?" Angel growled. "We just arrived. We couldn't have killed these people."

The young vampire pointed to Niccolo. "I saw you. As plain as day."

"As my friend said, we've just arrived." Niccolo nudged Angel out of the way and pressed his forearm against the vampire's throat. "Now tell us your name."

"Stefan," was all he said.

"Look at me, Stefan. If we did this, wouldn't we be covered in blood?"

Stefan nodded. His gaze darted back and forth between the older vampires before visibly relaxing.

"Stefan, it's a bit baffling to me that you survived this after what we've witnessed. How is that, and why do you think I was responsible for this?"

"I ... I hid," Stefan stuttered, his face red with obvious shame.

Angel had questions as well. "No one sensed you? This is the work of more than just rogues; there were shifters here and you mean to tell us that they didn't catch your scent?"

"They ... they knew I was here, at least I think they did. I think they wanted me to watch. Oh, God, they took Elsa and I just watched like a damn coward!" Stefan buried his face in his hands and began to cry.

It made Niccolo a bit uncomfortable to see this man break down this way. In human years, the young vampire didn't look a day past eighteen, but Niccolo knew he was much older. "How old are you, Stefan?"

"Eighty-five. I've run this office for nearly fifty years. These people didn't deserve to die like this."

"Did the attackers say anything?" Angel asked.

Stefan's brow furrowed like he was thinking really hard. "One of them looked toward my hiding place and said, 'This is only the beginning.' Then ... he said something weird: 'We shall inherit the earth.' What did he mean?"

Angel looked at Niccolo. "Is it just a coincidence that this place is owned by a vampire? What about the other sites?"

Niccolo's brain kicked into gear. What was going on? Had they just landed in the middle of some big conspiracy?

"Tell me, Stefan, why did you think I was already here?" Niccolo still wanted an answer.

"There was a vampire who looked just like you. He had your coloring and build. I thought ... but I suppose there were some differences."

"*Dio!*"

"Jagger?" Angel guessed shrewdly.

Niccolo didn't answer. He wanted to deny it, but had to face facts. Stefan's testimony, coupled with the scent Niccolo had picked up earlier, pretty much confirmed Jagger's presence. "Let's get the hell out of here before someone else stumbles on this scene. Stefan, you're coming with us."

<><><><><>

Sasha looked at her watch. Where the hell had Yuri gone? After a fruitless search through the city, they had returned to Wolf's. He'd said he would only be gone for a minute, but more than twenty had passed. She paced the floor of the sitting room.

She was beside herself with worry about Jagger. It was frustrating that no one seemed to know what was going on. And yet, despite her anxiety for her son, she couldn't stop thinking about Niccolo.

Seeing him again after all this time was torture, especially when she still had feelings for him. She wished she could stop loving him and maybe then she could stop suffering. Even if he was still entrenched within the enchantment spell, she hated that he refused to see the truth. It was beyond ridiculous that he still believed she created the spell. More like he had put *her* under a spell! Her hundredth birthday couldn't come fast enough. When it did, things would be much different. Her father would no longer be able to hold her powers hostage. And then she'd cast a spell on herself to chill her heart toward Niccolo Grimaldi.

Yuri entered the room. "You seem deep in thought, little one. I think that your concern is not just for your son—you are thinking about his father, perhaps?" She turned to face him and sighed. Although he had been a good friend to her, she didn't think Niccolo was any of Yuri's business.

"It's not important. What took you so long?"

"I'm sorry for the delay. I had to contact a couple of business associates. You should probably get some sleep. Your eyes are bloodshot and I bet you haven't rested well for days."

"I haven't, but I won't relax until Jagger is found."

"You're no use to him if you pass out from exhaustion, Sasha. There are many rooms here; why not take advantage of them? We haven't heard anything from the others yet. If you take a quick nap, you'll feel refreshed."

What he said made sense, but she didn't want to sleep. She wanted to go back out and continue searching for her son.

"You are dead on your feet. Do you think Jagger would want you in this state?"

"Okay, maybe I will lie down for a little while." Yuri was right; she was useless if she didn't get some rest. Sasha was so tired she could barely think straight.

He took her hand and she allowed him to lead her down a long narrow hall to one of the rooms. It was dark and had a large bed in the middle. Yuri shut the door behind them.

"Thanks, Yuri. You've been wonderful, but you can leave now," she murmured tiredly.

"I can be an even better friend, Sasha. You know how I feel about you." The hypnotic tone of his voice penetrated her mind, "Here, let me get you out of these clothes and then get you under the covers." The compulsion to comply was strong.

His fingers were already working on the buttons of her blouse. "Yuri… she offered a token protest.

"Shh, I'm just helping you out of your clothes. You know I won't do anything you don't want me to." Her shirt was off, and he began to undo her slacks.

She stared at Yuri, her mind oddly cloudy. Damned if he didn't look like Niccolo in that moment. Sasha stepped out of her pants and moved to get on the bed, but to her surprise, he pulled her against him.

"I've wanted to do this for so long. Just one kiss is all I ask," he said before he pressed his lips against hers.

Sasha stood motionless from surprise and fatigue. His kiss grew more insistent as his grip tightened on her, bringing her closer. Out of sheer curiosity, she wrapped her arms around his neck and returned his kiss. She had to know if she could feel something for someone other than Niccolo. Her lips parted under the probing of Yuri's tongue. She gave her all to that kiss and pressed her body to his. His mouth moved hungrily over hers.

She felt nothing, not even a slight stirring between her legs. Yuri's kiss didn't even approach what she felt when she was in Niccolo's arms. She tried to push away from him, but he held her tightly.

"Yuri, no. Let me go." She placed her palms against his chest.

"I burn for you, Sasha. Please don't tell me no." He dipped his head again. She turned her head away as his kiss landed on her cheek.

She didn't have a chance to respond before the door burst open. "What the hell is going on?"

"Niccolo!"

His amber eyes were glowing and he looked very pissed.

## Chapter Nine

Niccolo was so furious that he could barely see straight. After the information they had gathered in Austria, he and Angel had decided to split up. Angel would take Stefan to Dante and Romeo. Niccolo was going to check on Sasha and see how she was holding up. However, the moment he had entered the house, he knew something was out of place.

There was no sign of Sasha and Khrushchev, but he thought he could hear the faint sound of their voices in the back of the house. Although he half-expected it, he was still surprised to find Sasha locked in Khrushchev's embrace. Sasha was practically naked, standing in only her bra and panties. When he burst into the room, she jumped out of the warlock's arms with a guilty expression on her face.

"I asked you a question. What the hell is going on here?"

"What do you think, Grimaldi? I thought you were the smart one of the family."

"What are you talking about, Yuri? Niccolo, this isn't what it looks like." She sounded desperate, and there was a look of bewilderment on her face.

Niccolo glared at them both. "So this is what you two have been up to since we've been gone. Did you make this place your love nest while no one else was around? I've been out looking for my son and you've been here spreading your legs?"

Sasha gasped, her face turning scarlet. "That isn't true! Yuri and I have been doing some searching of our own. We've only been back for a short time ourselves."

"But I see you've managed to find something else to occupy your time with."

Sasha looked imploringly at Khrushchev. "Yuri, tell him the truth. This isn't what it looks like."

The warlock laughed. "Darling, there's no need to hide our love from this vampire. Who is he to you, anyway, but a sperm donor? Really, Grimaldi, you should learn to knock."

"Liar! How could you?" She brought her hand back and smacked Khrushchev across the face.

Niccolo wasn't buying the outraged virgin act from her. He had eyes, and he knew what he saw. He would deal with her later. Right now he couldn't ignore the warlock any longer.

"They have a saying in America, Khrushchev, and I think you should heed these words carefully: don't write a check that your ass can't cash."

Khrushchev threw his bead back and laughed. "How quaint. Was that a threat, Grimaldi?"

"If you knew me, you'd know that I don't make threats — I follow through."

"That's pretty big talk for someone who doesn't have his brothers to back him up this time."

"I don't need them to take care of you," Niccolo countered. Who the hell did this guy think he was? From the moment he had met Khrushchev, Niccolo had wanted nothing more than to tear this bastard apart piece by piece. This time he was through practicing restraint.

"Both of you, stop this! This was totally innocent, Niccolo, now leave me alone. And Yuri, I don't know what has gotten into you, but I don't like it one bit. Get out!" She had thrown her clothes back on.

Niccolo snorted in disgust. "There's no need for you to pretend. I know what I saw."

"Then you should have seen me trying to push away from him!"

He was too angry to take in what she'd said. "What kind of woman are you? Are your carnal needs more important than what's going on with our son? You didn't even ask what I've found out."

"You didn't give me a chance! You came in here throwing accusations at me like I'm some kind of tramp. I'm not a liar. If I wanted to be with Yuri, we would have already consummated our relationship. Trust me, we've had plenty of opportunities. She stood in front of him, hands on hips, five-foot-three inches of fury. "Go puff your chest out somewhere else, Niccolo, because I don't need this shit right now."

Khrushchev smirked. "Yes, Grimaldi, why don't you leave me and my woman alone?"

That was it!

Niccolo pushed Sasha aside and slammed his fist into the warlock's face. Khrushchev reeled back, but immediately regained his feet, catching Niccolo on the side of his face. As punches went, Nico had had worse, but it was enough to make him lose his balance and fall back.

"Stop it!" Sasha screamed at the top of her lungs, but both men ignored her.

Niccolo landed a blow to the warlock's stomach, making him double over. The next second, a bolt of light crashed into him, sending him flying across the room. His chest felt as though it were on fire from the blast.

He was back on his feet in an instant, charging at the laughing warlock, who shot another bolt of light. This time, however, he was prepared and dodged it. Niccolo flew at Khrushchev and tackled him to the floor. They thrashed around and finally ended up against a wall.

The warlock brought his hands up to thrust Niccolo away, but his strength was no match for the enraged vampire.

Niccolo was on top of Khrushchev and dug his fingers into his enemy's hair before pounding his head onto the floor. As he continued to slam the warlock's head up and down, he felt his chest begin to heat up. He looked down and saw that Khrushchev's hands were glowing, burning a hole into his shirt with their searing heat.

He ignored the pain and knocked the warlock's head even harder into the floor. Blood trickled down the side of his opponent's mouth. Niccolo jolted forward as something landed on his back.

"Stop it, you'll kill each other!" She yanked at his shoulders and tried to pull him off, but he was unyielding.

Niccolo shoved her off with one hand. Unfortunately, his temporary distraction gave the warlock just enough room to send Niccolo back with a glancing blow, then follow up with a knee to his groin. Niccolo howled in pain and fury.

He was tired of playing games with this bastard; it was time for him to die. His incisors descended and he leaned over and bit a large chunk of flesh from the warlock's neck and spit it back into his face. Blood splattered in his face.

Khrushchev screamed in agony and removed his hands from Niccolo's chest to cover his neck. The coppery scent of blood increased Niccolo's bloodlust. He wiped his eyes and smiled down at the warlock. "Do you have anything to say before you die?"

"Fuck you, Grimaldi. You're so damn smug now, but you won't be so cocky when *he* comes for you."

Niccolo hesitated. "What are you talking about?"

116

"You and all of your brothers will die — I hope he kills *you* first."

Before Niccolo could respond, a bright flash of light temporarily blinded him.

Khrushchev was gone.

"How could you? What the hell do you think you were doing?" Sasha demanded. She sat on the floor, her expression one of bewilderment.

Niccolo hovered over her, slowly licking the blood from his lips. Khrushchev's blood tasted foul. Niccolo knew that warlocks could only teleport short distances at a time, but Khrushchev was probably far enough out of his reach now that it was no longer worth the chase. *Coward.*

Niccolo ignored her question. "Do you know what he meant?"

She shook her head. "I have no clue. He's never acted this way before so I'm just as shocked as you are."

"Are you really?"

She frowned. "How can you ask that? Of course I am."

"Get up. I want answers now. Why was your friend at the airport when we arrived?"

Sasha slowly made it to her feet and moved away from him. "I don't know what you're accusing me of, Niccolo, but you can shove your goddamn accusations up your ass. I did nothing wrong!"

"And the fact that I found that bastard pawing you while you stood in his arms half-naked was innocent? Are you really telling me I didn't see what I did? Was it just an illusion? Or was I imagining things when you flung yourself on my back to protect your lover?" He cocked a brow in disbelief.

"I was trying to get you both to stop! I don't want either one of you fighting."

"Then why did you let him kiss you, hold you? Explain to me the touching little scene I witnessed." He stalked toward her with slow, deliberate steps.

Her eyes widened as she took a step back. "Stop this now, Niccolo."

He didn't answer as he continued to walk toward her, until Sasha was pressed against a wall. Niccolo reached out and spanned her throat with his hand. Once again the feeling he got whenever he was near her was beginning to take over. Her sweet fragrance drifted to his nostrils. Niccolo felt the need to take her into his arms and bury his cock so deep inside of her that they would both be lost in a wave of pure ecstasy. He aligned his body against hers.

*Just one taste,* he told himself, *and maybe I can get over this madness.* He lowered his head until their lips almost touched, but she twisted her head away.

"Your face is splattered with blood," she hissed. "It's disgusting."

He grabbed her chin and turned her head back toward him. "Blood that I have shed for you."

"You didn't shed blood for me. You went after Yuri because of your damned ego."

He ignored her words. "Damn, I must be crazy. My son is missing, danger surrounds us as we speak, yet I can't stop thinking about fucking you into submission."

"Too bad you'll never get the chance."

A grin curved his lips. "You don't think?"

"No," she protested.

"Yes. Woman, you have no idea what you've put me through."

She gave him a surprisingly strong shove and managed to duck away from him. "What *I've* done to you? How about what you've put me through?"

"You—"

"No! I will have my say and you had better listen to me well, Niccolo Grimaldi, because I won't repeat myself. Thirty years ago, I fell in love with you. Your warmth and understanding about my family situation made me feel that even if you couldn't return my feelings, we could at least be friends. Then you fell for Petra. Maybe I could have lived with that, but there were more forces at work than I realized at the time."

"What do you mean?"

"You once said Petra couldn't have cast a spell on you. Well, you were right, although I honestly thought she had at the time. If she had been the one who'd initiated the enchantment spell it would have ended with her death."

"Who, then, if it wasn't you or her?"

"My father. Blade told me what he'd done. It must be another reason for my father and brothers' falling out. I think the only reason my father confided in him was because he believed that he could involve Blade in his plot, about which no one will give me any answers."

"Why would he cast a spell on me? It makes no sense."

"I have never been one of my father's confidantes, but I have a feeling that it has something to do with this." She raised her palm to reveal a blood-colored birthmark that was shaped like a wildflower.

Why hadn't he noticed it before? Now that he thought about it, she'd always held her hands behind her back or clenched in front of her. "What is that?"

"It's the sign of Hecate. Those born with this sign are said to carry great power. Unfortunately, though I bear this mark, I have never displayed any great abilities. As far as my power is concerned, I've been a mediocre witch at best." A self-deprecating smile appeared on her face.

"What does this mark have to do with your father and me?"

"I think he's always resented me because of this mark. He also knew how I felt about you. Everyone did. But he wanted you and Petra, the favored child, together, for reasons I'm not quite sure of. When I told him I carried your child, he was furious, yet that didn't stop him from trying to take my son away from me. He told me that although I was the wrong daughter, the end result would remain the same. I still don't know what he meant by that." She took a deep breath. "I fought hard to keep Jagger. I wrote you not long after I found out I was pregnant, but you never responded. I could only believe you really meant those words the morning after Petra died."

"I received no letter!"

"I wouldn't lie about something this important, Niccolo. I wrote, but after two years of raising him alone, I realized that not hearing from you was probably a blessing in disguise. You had your brothers and the Underground, and I had Jagger. I appreciate the fact you've supported us financially, and I wish that you two could have had time together, but there's no point in wallowing in regret now. You're not the same person I loved and respected. My point is that while you have rights regarding your son, you have no rights where I'm concerned!"

Niccolo flinched. He noticed she had used the word "respect" in the past tense. He remained silent as she continued to speak.

"I don't know the specific spell my father used that not only made you fall for Petra but also gave you a disgust for me, but you no longer have to worry about my feelings. Once we find Jagger, I never want to see you again."

She turned away.

Niccolo couldn't let it go. "Why were you here with Khrushchev?"

"I've already said that's none of your damn business." She refused to look at him as she opened the door. "Clean yourself up, Niccolo, you're a mess."

## Chapter Ten

Dante pushed "End" on his cell phone, then raked his fingers through his hair. Having gone two nights without sleep, the vampire was feeling fatigued. "That was Nico. He's waiting for us back at Wolf's house. He thinks he has some useful information."

"Was it wise to let that young vampire go off by himself?" Romeo asked as he leaned against the wall of the hotel room.

"Carter and Angel are on it. They'll shadow the young one for a few days to make sure he's safe and doesn't try anything foolish."

Wolf excused himself from the room. "I need to make a couple of phone calls. I'll be back in a few minutes."

Dante remained silent as he watched the other vampire leave.

"What did Nico say? There's something you're not telling us," Romeo guessed shrewdly.

"I wanted to wait until we were back in Munich, but I suppose I can't keep any secrets from you." Dante smiled faintly. "That young vampire Angel brought to us fits into the overall puzzle that gets more complicated with each new piece. The massacre sites all had something in common. Stefan's office building, the apartment building, and the nightclub — all of these establishments were owned by immortals. That doesn't sound like a coincidence to me. This band of rogues is deliberately targeting these places — why?

You can't pick up a paper now without reading about these bloody scenes ... I believe they'll only get worse."

"Probably. I have a sinking feeling the Council has something to do with this. Don't you think it's suspicious that Devlin Locke has been elected as head of the Council? That pompous ass doesn't know shit. He's only a puppet—when we find out who's been pulling his strings, we'll likely find our answers."

"Perhaps, but what bothers me most about this whole situation is Jagger's involvement. Stefan swore there was a vampire in his office building who looked just like Nico."

Romeo shook his head. "Damn, what has that boy gotten himself into?"

"Nico is concerned he hasn't had first blood."

"You're kidding me."

"I'd never jest about something so serious. Apparently when Sasha last saw him, she thought he seemed a little feverish."

"*La morte dolci,*" Romeo muttered.

"Yes, and I fear that despite his mixed heritage, if he is in the later stages of his illness, he could be quite capable of the acts we have seen."

"Poor Nico. He must be torn up over this. Sasha as well."

"That's another thing. Sasha's friend Khrushchev is also involved in all this."

"How?" Romeo clenched and unclenched his fist. "I hope Nico took care of him. I knew there was something I didn't like about that bastard."

Dante recognized that look. His younger brother was raring for a fight.

"He made certain threats toward us. Nico finds it odd that Khrushchev just happened to be at the airport when he and Sasha arrived."

"It did seem rather convenient, didn't it? But how did he know they would arrive there?"

"Maybe Sasha isn't as innocent as she appears." Dante wanted to be wrong about that more than anything because he knew how Nico felt about her. Anyone with eyes in their head could see it. Until now, he had respected his brother's privacy and had not tried to analyze the situation between Nico and Sasha.

It was he who had sent Niccolo and Romeo to Russia thirty years ago. Although the mission had turned out to be fruitless and Romeo had returned, Nico had decided to stay. His younger brother had said he'd found someone to settle down with. Dante knew more than anyone that when vampires fall for someone, it is instantaneous, so he had wished his brother well.

Dante had met the entire Romanov family before, and Ivan, the head of the family, was beyond arrogant. Dante had liked the three sons but was conflicted about the daughters. No two sisters could have been more different in looks and personality. Although Petra embodied physical beauty, it appeared to be all surface, whereas Sasha's beauty had been deeper. It had surprised him when Nico had confessed his love for the beautiful but self-centered Petra. Of all his brothers, he would never have expected Nico to fall for a woman like her.

Nico never spoke of the events surrounding neither her death nor the circumstances of Jagger's conception, so Dante had left the topics alone. Through the years, however, he had kept tabs on his nephew and regretted that he didn't know Jagger better. He had not understood his brother's reasons for staying away from Jagger, but now, as more complications arose, Dante realized he would have made the same decision as Nico.

The danger had encompassed all the Grimaldis, and he admired Nico for having made such a difficult sacrifice. Dante also admired Sasha. It took a strong woman to raise a child on her own. When Dante had seen Sasha again, he'd known her main concern was for her son. No, she wasn't involved in this conspiracy. He had been crazy to suggest it.

Romeo must have thought so, too. "No. She's not involved in this. And by all accounts Jagger is a good guy. This doesn't seem like something he would be involved in, even though all evidence points to his participation. The entire situation is beyond disturbing."

"Believe me, Ro, I've gone over this a thousand times and my guess is as good as yours. We should head back to Wolf's and put our heads together."

"Do you think this has to do with *Il Diavolo?*"

"Without a doubt."

Sasha had never been more confused. Why would Yuri tell lies about the two of them? Something fishy was going on. He had been the one to initiate things, and he had been acting strangely from the moment they had met at the airport. Her mind was much clearer when he wasn't around. And while Sasha thought he deserved his beating for his lies, she didn't wish his death. Niccolo, on the other hand, was a whole other story altogether.

He was acting like a jealous lover. The way he had burst into the room with a proprietary air had incensed her, but on a baser level, it had also excited her. She was furious with both men and herself for losing focus of their goal, but even more disquieting was Yuri's threat.

He'd said Nico and his brothers would die. A strange sense of déjà vu suddenly hit her. *You remain alive to send a message, little witch. Niccolo Grimaldi and everything and everyone he holds dear will die.* Sasha shook her head. Three decades ago, the head rogue had spoken those words before he'd given a quick blow to her head and knocked her out. When she'd awakened, there was blood everywhere, and Petra's body had been ripped to shreds.

It sent a chill down her spine to think that Yuri could be involved in these killings, especially when she had allowed him so closely into her life. She'd thought that he was her friend, but after his actions she wondered. Sasha no longer believed their meeting at the airport was a coincidence.

She had been so grateful for his presence she hadn't stopped to think about why he was there. Sasha didn't want to believe someone she had called a friend would be involved in a plot to take out her son's father, but what other explanation could there be?

She now realized that when Yuri had gone out with her to search for Jagger, he'd deliberately thrown roadblocks in her way. When she'd wanted to go one way, he'd convinced her to go another. He also had told her that he'd had a vision of Jagger being in a particular building, but when they went there, it was empty. It seemed like they went from one dead end to the next. Sasha was now positive that Yuri had taken advantage of her powerless state. Just as it was apparent to her, he'd used his powers of suggestion to get her into bed. It chilled her to the bone to realize the person she'd thought was her friend was only in her life to spy.

"Please let my baby be safe," she spoke to no one in particular.

"We'll find him." Niccolo walked into the sitting room, and her foolish heart missed a beat at the handsome picture he made. He'd obviously showered, as he wore a change of clothes and his hair was still damp. His tight black jeans showed off the large bulge of his cock, and the white button-down shirt with the top two buttons undone revealed tufts of dark hair on his chest. Her mouth watered as she thought about pressing her mouth to the smooth column of his throat.

Sasha shook her head to rid herself of the lustful thoughts invading her brain. "Thank you. Niccolo —"

"If you're going to apologize for what you said earlier, don't bother. I deserved it."

"But I shouldn't have said it the way I did. Look, as someone pointed out earlier, emotions are running high and sometimes our mouths get ahead of our brains."

"That's true, but I had no right to come down on you the way I did. I will, however, caution you on the friends and lovers you keep."

"I knew nothing of his plans. I thought he was here to help, not antagonize you and your brothers. I ... apologize for his threats against you."

"Why? You had nothing to do with it."

"No, I didn't, but had I not insisted he come with us, none of this would have happened. I wonder how involved he is in Jagger's disappearance." She pressed her hands to her mouth. "Oh, God, what a fool I've been! I trusted him."

Niccolo's compassionate look made her snap. It was as if the floodgates were let open as a sob escaped her lips and tears streamed down her face. In an instant, he was at her side, his arms going around her. She gave in to the warmth of his embrace, leaning her head against his broad chest. All the misery that had been stored within her flowed out: her missing son, her strained relationship with her father, her lost sister, and her unrequited feelings for Niccolo. It was all so overwhelming.

"Shh, it's okay," he said, gently stroking her hair. She thought she felt his warm lips at her temple. She looked up at him. "Why are you looking at me like that?" he asked.

"Why are you being so nice to me?" Only a couple hours ago they'd been yelling at each other and she would have sworn he hated her.

"I thought a lot about what you said. I don't know why your father would put a spell on me, but if I am under a spell, he would be the only one old enough to do so without me realizing it. I asked myself why I was blaming you when I knew you couldn't be responsible. Maybe I've wanted you all along. This hardly makes any sense to me either, but I know how I feel at this moment." His amber eyes bore into her with an intensity that took her breath away.

Could this be a dream? Was he actually saying the words she had longed to hear for so many years? "But the spell ... I don't understand."

"Neither do I, but perhaps the time we've been spending together is cutting through it. When this is all over, I'm going to see your father to discover his reasons for doing this."

"I've always wondered why he would do this to us, but he never said. My father plays his cards very close to his chest." She sighed in frustration, and then realized she could feel the heat of his body. Niccolo's thigh was pressed against hers. Sasha bit her bottom lip.

"Don't do that. Your lips are too pretty to gnaw on like that." He leaned over her.

Sasha pulled back just before his lips met hers. Standing up abruptly, she began to pace. "This is very sudden. Your complete about-face is confusing."

"Like I said, I've done some thinking and I've come to the conclusion that there's no point in fighting this thing we have for each other." He stood up and walked over to her with slow deliberate steps, his gaze never leaving her face.

"No, Niccolo. We need to look for Jagger."

"We have to wait for the others to return." He paused. "Sasha, I've been a fool for the way I treated you before as well as the past few days. I badly wanted to touch you, taste you, hold you, but denied myself. I know I should be thinking about our son, but I want to fuck you, *strega*, fuck you desperately. I've almost driven myself insane with the need for you. I know I will go mad if I don't have you now."

Sasha was so astonished by his words that she didn't resist when he took her into his arms and his mouth came down on hers.

<><><><><>

"Come, young one. You're dragging your feet again." The older vampire beckoned Jagger into the modest house. With its green shingles and large bay windows in front, it was big without being ostentatious. Jagger could imagine a family living in this house, except it seemed so out of place as it was in the middle of nowhere.

What was so important that the redhead insisted they come here? The more he thought about it, the more uneasy he became. Things were just not adding up. This vampire who claimed to be his father was nothing like he'd expected. He'd heard how fierce the Grimaldi brothers were, but they weren't known to take out innocent people, only rogues. Then there was the cloudy feeling he got in his head whenever he questioned his father's motives. It was like being under a spell, but that couldn't have been possible because his father was a vampire. Magic was only something witches and warlocks were supposed to possess.

He cursed himself for turning back after witnessing the sickening atrocities of the previous nights. As horrific as the massacres had been, what bothered Jagger the most was the nonchalance in which these acts were committed. This vampire was off. A psychopath by human standards. Yet Jagger felt a slight connection to this older vampire. There was

129

no doubt in his mind they shared a bloodline but it wasn't the deep connection of father and son.

"Why are we here?" Jagger demanded, angry at the thought of being duped.

The older vamp turned glowing amber eyes on him, revealing his annoyance. "You ask too many damn questions."

"And you don't answer enough of them."

The redhead looked surprised. A slow smile spread across his face. "Your cockiness is very much like your…"

Jagger's eyes narrowed. "My what?"

"Never mind. Come, the meeting is about to start."

Again, his mind felt cloudy as he followed the older vampire into the house. He was a fool to follow this very dangerous vampire, but his need for answers outweighed his common sense. They walked down a narrow hall into what looked like a living room although it was spare of furniture. A steel coffee table sat in the middle of the room, and a few chairs were scattered around the hardwood floor -- occupied by the very men who'd participated in the earlier massacres.

"Welcome to my home, Grimaldi." A tall, painfully thin vampire with short brown hair walked toward them. He was pale like a zombie. Jagger didn't like him on sight.

He turned to the redhead … no matter what connection there was between them, Jagger couldn't bring himself to think of this man as his father. "What is going on?"

"We're planning our next strike. Roger here was kind enough to open his home to us. The least you can do is show a little common courtesy."

Jagger ignored the last bit. "Next strike? As I said before, I want no part of this. There is no reason at all for you to harm innocent people who are unable to defend themselves."

One of the men sitting in the corner chuckled. Jagger recognized him as the sadistic shifter who'd killed the little girl. Bastard. "Perhaps you need to show your *son* who's boss around here."

The emphasis on "son" was not lost on Jagger. Now he definitely knew something wasn't right. Father or not, he had to get out of here. He should have listened to his instinct and fled. The sense of impending doom jolted him into action. As he turned to go, he felt a pain in his head so intense it brought him to his knees. *What the hell?* He shook it off. It took him a moment to get back to his feet and when he did, he turned around to see a malevolent gleam in the redhead's eyes.

"Stupid boy. You were fun to toy with for a while, but now I've grown bored with you. Roger, as our host, I will give you a crack at wiping out Grimaldi's spawn."

For the first time in several days, Jagger could see clearly — think clearly. This man was not his father; the rogue had performed some mind-altering spell on him.

Black magic.

Jagger didn't know if he had any hope of getting out of here in one piece, but he wouldn't give up without a fight. "Who are you?"

"Adonis."

"Adonis who?"

"That's all you need to know."

"I suppose you won't tell me why."

Adonis laughed. "No, I won't." He turned to Roger, who eyed them with a gleam of eager anticipation. His incisors were bared as though he was ready for action. "He's all yours."

As Roger stalked towards him, Jagger threw his hand out in the direction of the steel coffee table. "Nostruis duemas sameud suutson!" The table shattered into long, slender shards, the metal pieces flying at Roger and piercing him through several points. The rest of the room's occupants ducked as the steel bits scattered all over the room.

Jagger felt his incisors descend; his fingers shifted to sharp claws, then he flew at the weakened rogue. Instinctively, he clawed into the screaming rogue's chest and ripped out his heart.

He watched as the life drained from the rogue, a surprised expression on the creature's face. Jagger was surprised, too. He'd never killed anyone before, but he knew if he wanted to get out of here alive, he'd have to do it again.

## Chapter Eleven

She tasted like heaven—so sweet and welcoming beneath his lips. He could feel her slowly responding to him as his he tightened his grip around her. It had been a long time since Niccolo had felt like this. Thirty years to be exact. He threaded his fingers through her silky, sable locks and massaged her scalp. His tongue ran across her bottom lip and savored the taste of her. Sasha released a soft sigh.

He could feel her body relaxing against his. Good. He wanted her to burn for him the way he did for her. "Open your mouth, Sasha. Let me taste you properly, sweetheart," he coaxed.

Sasha parted her lips a little wider, allowing him to slip his tongue inside. He explored her sweetness, reveling in the way she tasted, smelled, and felt in his arms. His cock stirred. He could feel a painful ache at the base of his balls. He needed her so badly.

Niccolo lifted his head to search her face. Her skin was flushed with passion and her dark eyes were filled with desire, and another emotion that made his breath catch in his throat— wariness. He had treated her badly and now she feared him. It tore at his heart. He knew he deserved it, but it still ripped at his insides. Damn Ivan for putting him through this.

"Sasha, I know you're uncertain of me because of the way we parted so long ago and by the way I've treated you upon our reunion, but I never stopped wanting you. I want you now. Need you."

"But you ... the spell ..." she began apprehensively.

"Perhaps I've been held prisoner by this enchantment spell, but it can't suppress my true feelings for you no matter how much I try to fight it. I want you so much right now I ache and you want me, too. Don't deny me, *strega mia*."

Her eyes widened. "Your witch?"

"Yes. My witch."

"But —"

"Don't talk. Let me taste you I hunger for you. Tell me that you want me, too."

"You know I do," she whispered, grabbing the sides of his face and pulling it back down to hers. "You have no idea how long I've waited for you to say those words to me." This time she was the aggressor. Sasha brushed her lips against his, pushing her tongue into his mouth. It darted past his teeth to swirl around his tongue and lick the inside of his mouth.

His body grew tighter with need at the exquisite sensations. The touch and taste of her was intoxicating. She pulled back and gave him a satisfied smile. "You are so beautiful."

"No, you're the beautiful one. Damn, I have to get you to a bed, because I want some pussy," Niccolo growled, before swinging her into his arms.

She let out a surprised yelp before wrapping her arms around him. He loved the way her head cuddled against his neck. The fruity scent of her hair was titillating. Niccolo licked his lips in anticipation as he practically ran through the house in search of an empty bedroom. He refused to make love to her where he had caught Yuri Khrushchev pawing her.

When he found a suitable bedroom, he walked in and placed her on her feet. He immediately began to unbutton her blouse. Niccolo was too damn hard to undress her with any finesse. He made short order of her shirt and bra. His gaze drank in the sight of her breasts, which were crowned with such red suckable nipples. His mouth watered to taste them, but he wanted to see every single inch of her creamy white skin first.

He pushed her hands away as she tried to help him remove her pants. He wanted to be the one to undress her. "No, let me," he said with determination.

"Only if you let me undress you."

"Okay, but I warn you, you had better be quick because my cock wants to be inside of you *now*." He hurriedly rid her of her remaining clothes and ripped off her panties.

Sasha gasped.

"You won't be needing these," he said as he discarded the torn underwear. His eyes fastened on her neatly trimmed cunt. He could smell the juices of her pussy -- the mouth-watering aroma made him want her even more.

Niccolo reached for her but she backed away. "Oh, no, you don't. You said I could undress you."

"I want some pussy," he said single-mindedly as he reached for her. He buried his face against the sweet-scented skin of her neck and ran his tongue over the pulse of her throat.

"Mmm, that feels wonderful, but I'm a little disappointed in you, Niccolo Grimaldi."

He lifted his head, eyes narrowed. "What are you talking about, woman?"

"I'm just trying to make you stick to the agreement. I want to undress you. Are you going back on your word?" She pouted, poking out her pretty bottom lip.

Unable to resist temptation, Niccolo lowered his head again to capture the protruding lip between his teeth. He nibbled on it before sucking it into his mouth, then released the tender flesh. Her hands clutched his shoulders and he felt her nails digging into his flesh.

"Oh, Niccolo," she moaned.

When he lifted his head, her kiss-swollen lips made him want to taste them again. "Be quick about this or I will take matters into my own hands," he warned.

She gave him a seductive smile, revealing small white teeth. It took all of his self-restraint not to fling her onto the bed. Her small hands began to work on his buttons. When his shirt was opened to the waist, she pressed her lips against his chest. The contact sent a shiver of pleasure down his spine.

"Do you like that?" she asked, before dipping her head to circle the flat disc of his hard nipple. He captured her head, holding it against his chest, wanting the delectable sensations coursing through his body to go on forever.

Niccolo cried out when her teeth nipped his sensitive nub. "You taste delicious," she murmured before transferring her attention to his other nipple. He stroked her head as her tongue darted back and forth over the hard little peak. Sasha's diligent hands undid the button of his jeans. Her dark eyes stared into his as she slowly slid down his zipper. She let out a let out a little gasp. "No underwear?"

"They're pointless," he answered through clenched teeth. His breath caught in his throat when she gently grasped his cock in her hands.

"Your cock is even bigger than I remember," she said with obvious delight.

He groaned. "Too much talking and not enough sucking my cock." Niccolo usually possessed more finesse in bed, but not where Sasha was concerned. His need for her was too strong to practice any real sexual etiquette.

She chuckled, seeming just as ready to make love to him with her mouth as he was to have her do it. As she slid his pants down his legs, she went to her knees.

He felt a sudden head rush at the warmth of her breath against his dick. Her tongue darted out to swirl around the head of his cock. It took everything in him not to thrust forward into her mouth. Sasha gently stroked his rod as she wrapped her lips around its tip. She moaned as she took his cock inch by inch of into her mouth. It felt wonderful.

The erotic picture of her dark head between his legs and her pretty red lips wrapped around him made Niccolo want to shoot his seed down her throat. Her mouth moved over his cock with an expertise that any courtesan would have been proud of. Rationally, he realized she had probably been with other men in the past thirty years, but the thought sent a wave of jealousy through him that made his body shake.

He took her by the forearms and hauled her to her feet. His cock bobbed up and down as it was pulled from her mouth. Niccolo seized a handful of her hair and tugged her head back, making her cry out.

"Who taught you to do that?" he demanded.

Sasha shot him a look of confusion. "What are you talking about?"

"Who are the other men you have been with? I'll kill them all!" A feral gleam lit his amber eyes.

The possessiveness in his look and tone of voice made her shiver. There hadn't been anyone else. She had dated and made out with other men, but none of them were Niccolo ... still, she didn't see why she should tell him that. He had no right to be angry if she had been with other men, but she knew there was no point in arguing with him. Besides, her body was so hot for his she could barely think straight.

"What about the women you've had?" she tossed back at him.

"Never mind that. How is it that you expertly sucked my cock? You were a virgin the first time we fucked."

"You can't expect a lady to reveal her secrets."

His eyes narrowed. It was obvious he didn't like the idea of her with other men. Good. Let him stew. It's no more than he deserved for trying to pull this macho act on her as if she were his property.

"Don't play games with me, Sasha. I want the names of every single man you've fucked since we've been together, and I won't leave this room until you do."

"Why should I tell you? You haven't been celibate. What gives you the right to expect that I was, too? Are you jealous that perhaps one of them was better than you?" The second she said the words she knew she'd gone too far. "Just forget about it, okay?"

"I want names." The very stillness of his voice made her tremble

"What would you do to them?"

"I'd make sure they learn never to touch what doesn't belong to them. You are mine."

Secretly his possessiveness thrilled her, but if she didn't soothe his jealously quick, things would get out of control. "You're being ridiculous."

"Give me the names, Sasha."

She now wished she'd never thought to make him jealous. "There hasn't been anyone else. I swear."

The look of suspicion on his face told her he didn't believe her. "Names."

"There were none! I've only been with you."

"Then, getting back to my previous question, where did you acquire your skills? You suck cock like a courtesan."

"Instinct."

"Instinct? Sasha, if you're lying to me —"

"It's true, I've ... I've dreamed about this moment and what I would do if we were ever together like this again."

"You dreamt all of this?"

"Yes. There's been no one else but you. You're the only man I've ever loved."

Niccolo cupped her face in his hand and looked into her eyes. "I know I'm being irrational. *Dio,* you have no idea how much I want you right now."

He covered her mouth with his again. Sasha loved the forceful way his lips devoured hers. She opened her mouth for the onslaught of his tongue, pressing the tips of her breasts to his naked chest. She was delirious with lust by the time he lifted his head. Her body felt as though it were melting.

"I can't hold off any longer. I need you now." He pushed her back on the bed before coming down on top of her. He spread her legs, and in the next instant his long, thick cock speared into her. He was so large that she momentarily felt pain, like it was her first time all over again. "*Strega mia?* Are you okay?"

He kissed her brow with a tenderness that made her heart flutter. She loved this man. Oh, how she loved him. "I'm fine; it's been a long time since I've had some wonderful vampire cock."

"I've found that I've developed a taste for witch pussy and yours is the best I've had so far." He moved his hips slightly, making her groan at the sensual feeling of him inside her.

"So far? Do you plan on trying other witch pussy?" She felt the little green-eyed monster rear its head.

"Are you jealous?" He lifted a dark brow as though she had amused him.

Sasha smacked his chest. "I'm glad you find this funny."

"Aww, don't be mad, sweetheart. I need to know —are you jealous?"

"Yes, damn you. There! Now you can laugh at me."

His expression turned serious. "I'm very pleased because I was very jealous when I saw you with that warlock. I wanted to rip him apart."

"You nearly did, but the scene wasn't what you thought it was."

"I realize that now, but let's not talk about him anymore. The only thing I intend to get into right now is this tight little pussy of yours." Niccolo rested his weight on his forearms as he pulled back and slid into her.

"Oh, God!" She felt a riptide of pleasure pulse through her. The discomfort was gone. Sasha loved the delicious sensation of his cock stretching the walls of her pussy to their limit. She lifted her hips to meet him thrust for thrust. "Fuck me harder!" she demanded, wanting him to brand her as his woman.

Niccolo glided into her harder and faster. Sasha wrapped her legs around his waist. One of his hands slid to her chest and caressed one taut breast. As his cock moved in and out of her, he rolled her nipple between his finger and thumb. "That feels so good," she moaned.

This was even better than the first time they had made love. Then, it had been a coming together of two people sharing a mutual grief. This time they were together because they both wanted each other. She burned for him, needing him more than air or food.

His cock was so deep inside of her he seemed to be piercing her to the deepest recesses of her body. She didn't know how but her body seemed made for his thick eleven inches. Sasha could feel the heat of her body rising as he picked up the pace. She could feel the juice drip from her cunt and she knew she was close to her peak.

"Damn, this is some good pussy, so juicy and wet. It smells tasty and, believe me, baby, I'm going to taste it," he warned.

"I'll hold you to it." She smiled up at him. Niccolo drove into her like a man possessed. She shivered when his eyes began to glow and his incisors descended. Sasha held her breath in anticipation of what was to come. He cupped her breast, never slowing down his pace.

Niccolo leaned down to sink his teeth into the soft flesh. She felt a slight prick when he pierced her skin. The sensation of his mouth sucking her blood and his cock fucking her cunt sent a wave of rapture through her body so intense she seized up and screamed his name over and over again. "Niccolo, Niccolo, Niccolo!"

*That's it, baby, let it out. Don't hold anything back.* The intimacy of his projected thoughts rushed through her.

Shortly after her own dramatic climax, he stiffened and she felt an explosion of his seed shoot into her hungry pussy. He lifted his mouth from her breast and kissed her.

The tangy flavor of her blood was on his tongue. He tightened his arms around her and rolled them on their sides, giving her another long, deep kiss.

She was in heaven. "That was amazing," she whispered, feeling drowsy.

"You were amazing."

As Sasha closed her eyes a content smile curved her lips.

## Chapter Twelve

Niccolo woke with the strangest sensation. Something felt off kilter. He shook his head, trying to figure out what it was. It took him a moment to remember where he was.

He felt a warm body next to his. Sasha. There was a look of contentment on her face, and her sleep seemed very peaceful. A smile curved her lips in her slumber. He moved a lock of hair from her forehead. She moaned and snuggled closer to him.

Despite the conflicting emotions which still warred within him, the more time he spent with Sasha he was inclined to believe she was indeed his intended all this time. That they'd spent so many wasted years apart cut him up inside. One thing he did know with absolute certainty was that he wanted Sasha more than he had ever wanted anyone else, including Petra. His body craved her and he would no longer deny himself the pleasure. As soon as he found Jagger, Niccolo planned to go to Ivan and demand that he release them from their respective spells and find out why the warlock had cast them in the first place.

His greatest wish, however, was to take back all the hurtful things he's said to Sasha. Being under an enchantment spell was of no consequence to him. He'd caused her pain and would make it up to her.

Niccolo licked his lips as he watched the sleeping beauty, wanting nothing more than slide into her tight pussy again. He had only tasted the coppery sweetness of her blood, but now his mouth watered in his need to sample her cunt and all its nectar. His dick was stiff as a board and he needed relief.

As he moved, the blanket dipped lower, revealing one pert red nipple that peeked out, tempting him to take it into his mouth. He rubbed his balls to alleviate some of the ache building up inside of him. He had to have her now or else he'd go insane with need. The delectable picture she presented was too enticing to resist. He lowered his head and captured the exposed tip between his teeth and sucked gently.

Sasha stirred but didn't awaken. Niccolo swirled his tongue over the nipple. A deep moan flowed from her throat. She rolled her head from side to side still in her dream state. Damn, she was hot. He licked and fondled her small breast, wishing she would wake up.

He pulled the blanket completely off and slid down the bed. He pushed her legs apart and positioned himself between her silky thighs. Niccolo pressed his nose against her neatly trimmed pussy, inhaling her essence. Her scent was intoxicating. Unable to go another second without eating her pussy, he licked her damp slit, gently at first. The taste of her immediately went to his head. With a growl, he parted her labia and dove in, thrusting his tongue into her channel.

He knew Sasha had wakened when she threaded her fingers through his hair and shoved her mound against his face. "Feels. So. Good," she moaned.

Niccolo slipped his tongue in and out of her wet channel, savoring every drop of her moisture. He caught her clit between his thumb and forefinger and gave it a light twist. She bucked her hips against him. He lifted his head then to take her throbbing button between his lips and suckled firmly. Niccolo then slipped two fingers inside of her thrusting them in and out, slowly at first before picking up the pace.

"Oh God, what are you doing to me?" She cried out, even though the grips she had on his hair didn't loosen. If anything she held him closer, fucking his face with her pussy. But

Niccolo loved every second of it. He loved how responsive she was to his ministration and he especially loved how wet her pussy got. His face was drenched in her juices and he couldn't get enough of it.

He nibbled on her clit until it grew plumper and she got wetter. When her body stiffened signaling the point of her release, he released her clit and fastened his mouth over her labia.

"Yes! Yes! Yes!" Sasha screamed her orgasm.

Niccolo greedily sucked her juices until there were none left. But he was not finished her. Rising to his knees he grasped his cock and guided it into her damp hole.

She wrapped her legs around his waist with a sigh. Niccolo lifted her lower body, sinking into her balls deep. Nothing ever felt more right. Being inside of Sasha was like giving his body much needed nourishment. His eyes locked with hers as he slowly moved. She bit her bottom lip as she moaned. *Dio*, she was beautiful.

The moved in sync, neither saying a word. Her cunt was so slick and tight, gripping him like warm, wet velvet. Niccolo prided himself on his stamina but with Sasha, he couldn't hold out for long. He exploded within her. "*Strega*," he grunted.

Sasha dragged her nails down the center of his chest and cried out as she climaxed. When he spilled the last bit of his seed, he collapsed on top of her.

They remained silent for several moments, his head resting against her chest. The beat of her heart pounded in his ear.

Sasha stroked his hair. "I wouldn't mind being woken up like that again." She giggled.

He lifted his head to smile at her. Her dark, lust-glazed eyes had shadows beneath them, and he almost felt guilty for waking her. Neither one of them had had much sleep within the past few days, but he was better equipped to handle it than she was.

Niccolo slipped out of her with regret and grabbed the blanket to cover her body. As he did this, he leaned over to give her a slow, lingering kiss on her lips.

"Mmm, that was nice. It doesn't seem like we slept for long. I feel like I just closed my eyes."

"According to the clock, you were only sleep for a half hour. Why don't you rest some more and I promise not bother you," he suggested.

"Now that I'm up, I probably won't be able to go back to sleep." She yawned and suddenly narrowed her eyes. "Something is bothering you."

Niccolo was surprised she was able to pick up on that, but then again, witches had strong intuition. "It's nothing."

"I now there's something. Tell me." The look of concern on her face made him want to confide in her, but how could he when he wasn't sure what exactly was bothering him? Sasha reached up to stroke his jaw. He closed his eyes, savoring the touch of her soft hand on his cheek.

He took her hand in his and brought it to his lips, kissing each finger one at a time. "As fabulous as that feels, you're not going to distract me from my question. Something is bothering you."

Niccolo sighed and sat up. "It wasn't a diversionary tactic, Sasha."

"Maybe not, but you don't seem to want to answer me."

"To be honest, I don't even know what's bothering me. I—" Suddenly the strange feeling that had awoken him was back. It left him panting for air.

Sasha clutched his arm, but he couldn't move. Then he heard a faint voice in his mind.

*Papa, I need you.*

The voice was stronger that time. Jagger!

"What's the matter? What's going on?" Sasha shook his arm.

*I can't hold them off much longer.* The voice grew fainter.

*Where are you?*

*Just outside of Salzburg, I think.*

*Hold on, son, I will come for you.*

Niccolo jumped out of bed. "Our son is in trouble," he said, donning his clothing as quickly as possible.

"Oh, my God. I'm coming with you." She scrambled out of bed and grabbed her discarded clothing.

Niccolo knew she had as much right as he did to find out what the trouble with Jagger was, but she would only slow him down. Time was of the essence. "Sasha, stay here. I am going to need to get where I'm going as fast as I can, and without your powers you won't be able to keep up with me."

"I won't be left behind. He's my son, too."

"And what will you do once we get there? You are helpless. These are dangerous people, and I can't worry about the both of you."

"I can take care of myself," she said with a defiant gleam in her eyes.

"No. I won't argue about this."

"You can't stop me from going."

He shook his head in frustration, pulling her into his arms. "*Strega mia,* I don't want anything happening to you. I care about you." He bent down to briefly press her lips with his. The sweetness of her mouth was tempting, but there was no time.

"But you don't love me, do you?"

"I don't know, but I want you to understand that I need and desire you so much that I ache. I also know that if anything were to happen to you, it would devastate me. The thought of losing you causes me a great deal of distress."

"Niccolo —"

He placed a finger over her lips. "By your own admission, your powers have been bound. I have a point and you know it."

She didn't look happy but nodded.

"Good. I need to leave now." He kissed the corner of her mouth.

"Please hurry and bring my baby back safe."

"I will, which is why I have to leave you behind," he said with a confidence he didn't feel. What if he *didn't* get to his son in time? The thought filled him with agony.

"Go," she implored, her eyes filled with unshed tears.

Niccolo nodded, before dashing out of the room. He raced out of the house calling out to Jagger. *I will be there as soon as I can, son. Be strong.*

Briefly he debated whether to take the motorcycle in Wolf's garage or to go on foot. When he ran, he could go much faster than most man-made vehicles, but the dilemma lay in transporting his son safely back here. No, he'd worry about transport on the way back. For now there was no time to delay. He paused for a moment to pull out his cell phone and quickly punched in his brother's number. He wasn't sure exactly how far Dante was away from him and didn't want to waste the time it would take to try and bridge a long distance to communicate with him telepathically.

"Dante here."

"It's Nico. I need your help."

"What's the matter?"

"Jagger is in trouble. He called out to me. I fear I may not make it to him in time."

"Where is he?"

"Just outside of Salzburg. Where are you? You feel close."

"I'm not too far from you, but I'm still closer to Salzburg. Romeo and Wolf are with me. We were heading back to Munich, but we'll go to Salzburg."

"Have someone watch over Wolf's place. I don't want to leave Sasha unprotected."

"I'm on it."

"Hurry."

"We will." Dante clicked his phone off.

Niccolo ran as fast as he could. He couldn't remember running so hard before except for the night so long ago when he'd raced to save Petra unsuccessfully. His heart felt as though it would burst from his chest, but he couldn't slow down. He had to get to his son.

Failure was not an option.

Jagger held out his hands to erect a barrier around him, silently praying he would be able to maintain it until help arrived. The immortals he faced were much older than he was, so there was no hope of besting them in a physical match.

His attackers beat against the invisible shield, unable to break through. He never would have imagined that his quest for answers would lead him to this, but if it was his time to go, he would die fighting. His biggest regret was not seeing his mother one last time.

*Papa, where are you?*

Perhaps it was instinct that had made him call out to his father. After all, if what his mother said about his father caring about him was true, and Niccolo was near enough to hear him, then he would come. Jagger figured he didn't have anything to lose. When he had received a response, the first glimmer of hope he'd felt in the last several days sprang forth. He thought he might actually survive this disaster after all, but with each passing second, hope faded.

Only days ago he had set out in search of his father and thought he had found who he was looking for. After leaving his mother's he had gone to a local bar, a known hangout for warlocks and other immortals. He'd figured others would know how to find the Grimaldis.

It wasn't long before someone gave him the information he sought. Jagger went back to his apartment to pack. He needed to find his father because only he could explain the changes he was going through as a vampire. He didn't know too much about the vampire physiology or lifestyle, so he didn't know if what he was experiencing was normal. Whatever it was, he ached and yearned so deeply for something that he could hardly breathe at times.

He had never been sick a day in his life, so how else could he explain this sickness? Jagger wanted answers—he *needed* answers. As he was about to board a plan to the United States, a stranger had approached him —a stranger with amber eyes like his claiming to be his papa. He'd initially been disappointed because he'd felt nothing for the cold stranger who stood before him.

"Come with me, my son, and I will give you the answers you seek," he had said.

Jagger had been reluctant to follow him, but then a haze fell over him. He suddenly focused on the fact that this vampire was his father. The thought was sudden and had seemed to come out of nowhere. He might not have known much about his vampire side, but he did know enough about magic to realize too late he'd been in this rogue's thrall.

What a fool he had been! He should have suspected that black magic had been at work, but his eagerness to find answers had blinded him — that and the spell. The horror and the massacres of the past few days had nearly destroyed him.

A big gray werewolf barreled against his barrier, then growled, baring large, menacing teeth. Blood ran down the side of the wolf's muzzle.

*You will die tonight,* the wolf projected. Jagger ignored him, concentrating on his barrier. It was getting harder and harder to hold onto it. His arms grew weaker, and his muscles quivered.

"Shit," he cursed.

"Surrender, Nikolai Grimaldi. Your time is up." The redheaded vampire laughed, his amber eyes glistening with amusement and malice.

Jagger glared at him. "You bastard! Tell me who you are!"

His adversary laughed again; the maniacal sound sent a chill down his spine. "You are not in a position to make demands, baby vampire. Do you think that puny barrier will stop us? I know a power much greater than yours," he taunted.

"Then why haven't you broken it? You're all talk."

"Brave words for one who will meet a painful death. You're just as cocky as the rest of your family — it will give me great pleasure to tear you limb from limb. Just imagine what it would do to your poor father." He smiled widely. "Isn't it laughable that while he thought he was protecting you all these years, we had in fact always known of your existence? We've been watching and waiting, young one. Your time has come. Did you know I had planned to save you for last? I was going to kill your uncles and your father, then you, but your stubbornness has earned you your death here and now."

"Why do you want us dead?"

The vampire ignored his question. "You have a lot of questions for someone in your precarious position, don't you? In most circumstances a little cockiness is admirable, but in a Grimaldi I find it sickening. Don't worry, Nikolai, soon you will have company in Hell when your family joins you there. It was fun seeing how far we could push you." He pointed to a nearby corpse. "It's almost a shame you killed Roger. He would have enjoyed seeing your demise. Well, the fun and games are over." The rogue charged at Jagger's barrier, which shook under the impact, knocking Jagger back.

He was going to break through! A second werewolf charged against the barrier and this time it wobbled. Jagger nearly lost his hold of it. He fell to his knees, feeling weak.

A tall, blond warlock entered the room, temporarily distracting everyone there.

Jagger cried out in relief. "Yuri!" He didn't know how he had come to be here, but Jagger didn't care. He was just so happy to see his friend.

"Khrushchev, you're late as always, but no matter, you are just time to witness some fun." The rogue smirked.

"Yuri?" Jagger was confused. What was going on? Why wasn't his friend helping him?

Yuri looked from Jagger back to the redhead. "You said he would not be harmed! When his grandfather finds out —"

"Ivan doesn't call the shots. I do. This is his lesson for getting involved with the Grimaldis in the first place. You would have thought he'd learned from the first time. Now, I'd advise you to watch your mouth before you're next." The vampire's amber eyes glowed.

Yuri took a step back. He looked conflicted and it twisted Jagger's gut to know that his so-called friend was a part of this mess. "Yuri, how could you? My mother trusted you. I trusted you!"

"Don't take it personally, Nikita. I ... I'm sorry." Yuri didn't even have the balls to look him in the eyes.

"You motherfucker!"

"Adonis, please. Can't you spare him? His grandfather is loyal to the cause. Jagger has no part in all this."

So that was the redhead's name!

Adonis eyed Yuri with contempt and raised one dark-red brow. "So you don't want to see the baby vampire die?"

"No. Spare him." Yuri kept his eyes downcast.

Adonis turned to the two wolves that had been snarling at Jagger. "Make it so our *friend* Mr. Khrushchev doesn't witness the baby vampire's death."

The shifters in the room sprang at Yuri so quickly the warlock didn't have time to react. One shifter lunged for his throat, the jaws locking onto Yuri's flesh before he could even let out a scream.

Jagger watched in horror as the weight of another shifted wolf knocked the warlock over. The second wolf bit into Yuri's chest, crunching past bone. The warlock screamed but no sound came out of his mouth as he fruitlessly tried to defend himself. A faint light emanated from his fingers, but Jagger could see that Yuri was too near death to be effective. The first wolf shredded Yuri's neck, while the other ripped open his stomach and began to feast on his entrails. Yuri's sightless eyes stared up at the ceiling as he lay dead.

Adonis faced the two rogues present. "Are there any more objections?" They quickly shook their heads. Jagger knew he was doomed.

Adonis charged at the barrier—and broke it. Jagger was thrown back. The older vampire pounced on him in a flash. He lifted Jagger off the ground and over his head, then threw him across the room.

Jagger hit the wall heavily before crashing to the ground. The other two rogues grabbed him by his arms and brought him back to his feet. He tried to break free, but they were too strong for him. Adonis slowly stalked toward him, menace lurking in the depths of his eyes.

"I have been waiting for a very long time to take out the Grimaldi brothers but, the son of one will do just fine for now."

Jagger kicked one of his captors and tried to free himself from their grasps. They held him tighter until he could barely move. Adonis's incisors descended and his now claw-like hands poised to strike.

"Any last words?" Adonis smirked.

He refused to give this bastard the satisfaction of pleading for his life. Jagger cleared his throat and hawked a thick loogie in the rogue's face.

Adonis snarled, his face turning a shade that nearly matched his hair. "I will enjoy killing you."

The rogue's hand came down and ripped into Jagger's chest. The pain was excruciating, but he refused to cry out. Adonis lifted his other hand, ready to give him another swift blow, when out of nowhere someone pulled him away from Jagger.

Through a cloud of agony, Jagger was surprised to see a new vampire standing behind Adonis. "It appears there is a party going on and we weren't invited."

Two more vampires rushed into the room to join the first. Jagger looked at the newcomers. One had dark hair like his own, and the other two had blond hair. The dark-haired one stepped forward. "I guess we're just going to have to crash it."

This time Jagger was sure the new arrivals were on his side.

## Chapter Thirteen

Dante surveyed the ugly scene in front of him and his heart nearly stopped. Two wolves were eating the remains of what looked like a man. A redheaded vampire he was sure he had seen before hovered over Jagger while two other rogues held his nephew's arms. He knew this was Jagger; he looked too much like Nico to be anyone else but his nephew.

"Grimaldi!" The redhead turned around with a look of pure venom in his glowing eyes—his Papa's eyes! Who the hell was this vampire? One of the wolves lifted his head and growled. The other followed suit as they circled him, Romeo, and Wolf.

Romeo hissed with obvious impatience. "Let's waste these bastards. What are you waiting for, Dante?" Dante held up his hand to silence his restless brother.

"Who are you?" Dante demanded, his fingers flexing at his side. He wanted to strike out but knew that one wrong move could end his nephew's life.

"Why, I'm the one you've been seeking. Looks like you've finally found me." The redhead sneered.

"*Il Diavolo?*" Dante couldn't believe after all these many years, he faced the rogue at last.

"*Il Diavolo?* Not quite, but close. Giovanni wishes he was as powerful as I. No. I'm not your weak *il Diavolo*, but I *am* your worst nightmare. Lazarus, Remus, attack!"

The two wolves sprang at Romeo and Wolf. Dante looked at the two rogues who held Jagger hostage. He could tell that he was much older than they were and he could probably take them without breaking a sweat. He moved swiftly, punching one in the face and delivering a kick to the stomach to the other. Temporarily stunned, they released Jagger, enabling Dante to grab his nephew and pushing him aside. The rouge recovered quickly and snarled at him with anger before they charged toward him. Dante ducked a fist that flew his way but was pounded in the chest by another. He staggered backward.

Instantly, the two rogues were on him with bared teeth. One swiped his clawed hand across Dante's face, making him grunt in pain. He wouldn't let them win—he couldn't—not when he'd finally come face to face with the vampire he'd sought for so long.

He brought his knee up and caught one of the rogues in the groin. The injured rogue howled. Dante thrust him away and dodged the other's fist, delivering his own punch. He heard the cracking of bones as he connected with the second rogue's face. By now, the other rogue had recovered and moved in to bite Dante, aiming for his jugular, someone jumped onto the rogue's back and sank his incisors into the rogue's neck.

It was Jagger. Dante could now concentrate on one rogue at a time. The rogue he'd attacked was on his knees, his face still healing. Dante didn't intend to let the bastard complete the process.

He grabbed the kneeling rogue by the collar and kicked him across the floor. The rogue crashed into the wall. Out of the corner of his eye, Dante checked to see how Romeo and Wolf were holding up. Romeo was laughing as he usually did in battle. Wolf's adversary had shifted back to human form and the two immortals wrestled on the floor. It looked as though Wolf had the upper hand when he thrust his fist into his adversary's throat and pulled out the man's tongue.

Dante saw his nephew struggling and knew he had to finish off his opponent quickly so he could help him. The redheaded rogue was nowhere in sight. What the fuck?

Before he could ponder that any further, his enemy tackled him to the floor. Dante cursed himself for allowing his attention to stray. The rogue wrapped his claws around his throat, the talons digging into his skin.

Dante could feel blood seeping into his throat. He dug his own claws into the rogue's face, eliciting another scream of pain from his enemy. The grip loosened around his neck.

A shout rang out from the other side of the room. Just as he feared—Jagger was not holding up well. The earlier attack had weakened him too much. The rogue dragged his talons down the front of Jagger's already bloodied chest.

In a desperate attempt to get to his nephew, Dante gouged his opponent's eyes out. The rogue shrieked and buried his face in his hands. Dante shoved him away, quickly stood up, and stomped the rogue's head, squashing it like a grape. He then leaned down and ripped the writhing vampire's chest open before pulling out his heart. Dante ripped the bloody organ to tiny pieces, ensuring the rogue's death.

He rushed over to his nephew's side and tossed the rogue away from him. He quickly looked over Jagger, whose breathing was ragged, his face pale and eyes clouded. "Jagger, are you okay?"

"Yes," he whispered, though Dante wasn't sure he believed him.

Dante turned back to the rogue he had thrown off of his nephew and breathed a sudden sigh of relief to see Nico flash through the door. Teeth barred and talons out, he flew at the rogue on the floor. Nico grabbed him by the neck and lifted him with one hand. His amber eyes glowed dangerously.

"This is what happens when you fuck with my son," he hissed.

The rogue struggled against Nico's grip but was no match for Dante's enraged younger brother. With his free hand Nico grabbed the rogue by the balls and ripped them off before stuffing them into the howling rogue's mouth. Then he jabbed his claws into his enemy's gut and split him wide open. The rogue's organs spilled out. Blood gushed everywhere. Nico threw the vampire on the ground and scooped up the heart, crushing it in his palm. Dante had never seen his brother so cold-blooded.

He looked over at the others. Wolf's opponent lay dead at his feet, and Romeo was still battling his werewolf. From the looks of things, the shifter was near death.

"Romeo, stop toying with him and finish him off." Dante wanted to leave father and son in peace.

Romeo glared at him. "You're no damn fun." He grabbed the wolf and yanked out his spine, then made short order of ripping the agonized wolf apart. Dante turned back to Nico, who stood frozen. He looked at his injured son with such longing that Dante's heart went out to him. "Will you be all right, Nico?

Nico nodded. Dante gave him a long, assessing look before signaling Wolf and Romeo to leave. He smiled at his brother and nephew in relief before walking out the door.

Niccolo looked at his son, who was kneeling over and clutching his chest in obvious pain. There was blood everywhere. He had always imagined that when he finally had a proper meeting with his son that it would be under much different circumstances, but here they were. He took a step forward. "Son..." he whispered, throat clogged with emotion.

An overwhelming mixture of love and longing washed through him. He wasn't sure how to act in this situation. Should he take Jagger into his arms and assure him things would be okay? Would his embrace even be welcomed?

Jagger's dark head shot up. He was so different from the little boy he had seen twenty-seven years ago. Amber eyes so like his own were tinged with pink. Blood dripped down the sides of his mouth.

"Who are you?" Jagger demanded through gritted teeth. It was obvious he was trying very hard not to show how much pain he was in.

"I'm your papa; can't you feel it?"

His son slowly got to his feet, eyes narrowed. "How do I know you are who you say you are? I've been fooled once already," he said, backing away.

"Can you look at me and deny who I am? Are you not my very image? You called out to me and I've come." Niccolo stepped forward, but Jagger retreated. There was a look of wariness in his son's eyes; he knew it was because of the horror of past few days.

"*Dio!* What have they done to you? They've twisted your mind, haven't they?"

"I ... I was on my way to find my father ... you. I needed answers I could no longer deny myself. At the airport someone approached me. He eyes like ours and said he was my father. I felt no connection with him at least not as one as deeply as a father and son bond should be, but then things became cloudy. It seems the last few days have been a blur to me. Obviously, black magic was involved, because that rogue was not my father."

"Damn right he wasn't, because I am. They hurt you; let me help you heal." Niccolo moved again, but Jagger held up his hand and Niccolo felt a shield blocking his path.

159

"Do not erect barriers against me."

"Under the circumstances, you must admit that it's a bit awkward for me to just fall into your arms."

"Then why did you seek me out in the first place?"

"Wouldn't you want answers if you spent nearly thirty years of your life without the presence of a father you knew was alive and well? Didn't you think I would wonder why you left my mother the way you did? She loved you, but you abandoned her and me. I've lain awake at night wondering why. Was I not good enough for you? Did you not want to deal with raising a half-breed?"

Niccolo knew his son was hurt and confused; he wished he could say something that would take away Jagger's pain. His son looked at him with such contempt that it sliced his insides. He would have rather faced a thousand rogues, knowing there was no possibility of victory, than to have his son look at him like that. "Whether you believe me or not, I never abandoned you."

"Liar!"

"It's true, son. I may not have been in your life like a father should have been, but I was always around, making sure you were safe, providing for you so that you never went without."

"Do you think material things matter to me? It was you I needed. You! Not your money or what you could provide. I've lived my whole life wondering what it is about me that kept you out of my life. Perhaps I could live with you not loving me, but I cannot get past how you treated my mother."

"Believe me when I say I love you so much that not a day has gone by when I haven't thought about you. It hurt to know you were growing up without me. I have pictures of every birthday party, every accomplishment. I have ones where your smile lights up your entire face, ones of you growing to manhood, and ones where you are in deep thought. Those are my favorites because I imagined you were thinking about me. When I look at them, it is almost as if you are right there with me, but the pictures have never been enough." He broke off. Jagger looked as though he was softening but the look of mistrust was still evident.

"I wish I could have been there, but your mother and I did what we thought was best. As you've learned these past few days, I have some very dangerous enemies, and the threat encompasses my entire family and those I love. It is why your aunt died. Your mother and I didn't think it was a good idea for me to be in your life. It's probably still not a good idea, but our relationship is in the open now. I won't allow you to shut me out. If you need me to get on my knees and beg your forgiveness then I will ... just don't turn me away."

Jagger looked at him with an unreadable expression in his eyes. Niccolo fell to his knees, pain piercing him so deeply he could barely gather breath. His head fell into his hands, tears dropping from his eyes. It was a familiar pain. He realized the last time he felt this was the night he'd walked away from the then two-year-old Jagger. It hurt far more than anything physical. "Don't ... shut ... me ... out," he pleaded.

When he received no response, his head shot up and he reached out to touch the barrier between them. "Perhaps you are too old to need me anymore, but I need you. I need you in my life very much, Jagger. I love you and I need you." He gently pushed against the shield, hoping his son could feel the love radiating from him.

"I ... what about my mother? How can I forgive you after you broke her heart? How could you do that to her?"

"I freely admit what I did wasn't right, but everything is not as it seems. There were other forces that kept us apart. However, within the past few days, your mama and I have been able to work out most of our differences. She's back in Munich and she's very worried about you. Please take down this barrier. Let me heal you. Let me take you in my arms and hold you like I've long to do all these years."

Still Jagger hesitated. There was a look of confusion on his face as though he couldn't make up his mind.

"One thing you will learn about me, son, is that I'll never lie to you. Now that I've found you again, you're not going to get rid of me."

"Again?" Jagger's golden eyes swam with unshed tears.

"Yes, again, son. When I learned of your existence, you were still a *bambino*, just two years old. I was so very proud of you. I wanted more than anything to take you with me. I didn't care you were only half-vampire. All that mattered was that you were mine and I loved you. You have no idea what it was like for me to walk away from you. Please ..." Niccolo pressed his hand against the barrier once more, and to his surprise it disappeared.

Jagger dropped to his knees and faced his father. He touched Niccolo's face in almost the same way he had when they had first met. Their eyes locked and he could feel his son warming toward him. "Papa?"

"Yes, son. I am here." He pulled Jagger into his arms. The younger man broke into sobs as he wrapped his arms tightly around his father. Niccolo was filled with such joy that he knew if he died at this moment, he would die happy. "It's okay, Papa is here. I'll never leave you again." He stroked his son's head and rocked him back and forth.

"Papa?"

"Yes, Jagger?"

"I hurt."

"I know. Let me heal you." He clasped Jagger's face in his hands. They spoke without words, communicating as only father and son could. After a while, Jagger seemed to understand. He nodded his head before his incisors descended.

Jagger leaned over and sank his teeth into the side of Niccolo's neck. Niccolo clutched Jagger's head against him as he fed.

Now, more than ever, he had to vanquish his enemies to keep Jagger and Sasha safe.

### Chapter Fourteen

Sasha waited anxiously for Niccolo to return. Although he had promised he would bring their son back to her safely, she couldn't help but worry. She hadn't been able to sleep a wink, and she was very angry that Niccolo had sent someone to watch her. The vampire barely spoke two words to her and stayed out of her way, which was a good thing.

At the sound of the door opening, her bodyguard sprang to his feet and pushed her behind him. She ran around him to the hallway. Her face fell when the tall, blond vampire Wolf walked in. She clutched his arm. "Where's Niccolo? Where is my son?"

"I almost envy them that they have a pretty little *fraulein* like you waiting for them." He winked at her.

"Back off, Wolf, before my brother kicks your ass." Romeo walked in with a smirk on his face. He winked at Sasha, too. "My brothers are getting out of the car. Jagger is with them."

"Oh, thank God!" She nearly fainted with relief. The two vampires grabbed her arms to steady her.

Dante walked through the door then, but she looked past him, anxious to see the two men of her heart. Niccolo came inside with his arm around Jagger's waist. Jagger was pale and his shirt was stained with dried blood.

"*Moy Malish!* My baby!" Sasha ran to him and threw herself into his arms.

*Eve Vaughn*

Jagger caught her, squeezing her tightly against him. "*Uspokoysya, vse khorosho,* Mama." He kissed the top of her head.

Tears of relief streamed down her face. "Yes, I know everything is okay now that I have you back safe with me. But you look a mess. What happened? Who hurt you? Have you been eating properly?"

"Mama, please, you have to let go of my neck, I can barely breathe." Jagger chuckled.

She released him as he placed her back on her feet. Sasha looked over at Niccolo and felt the old excitement rushing through her veins. No matter how many times she saw him, he still had that effect on her. She suddenly felt shy, remembering what they had shared earlier, and how delicious his cock had felt inside of her, and the forcefulness of his kisses and caresses against her skin. She wasn't sure how she was supposed to act now. For so long she had lived thinking he didn't care, and even though he had finally admitted that he did, he had never said he loved her.

"What? No hug for me?" Niccolo lifted one dark, sexy brow, and opened his arms. She looked at Jagger with uncertainty. Her son gave her a little smile of encouragement.

She turned into Niccolo's arms. He, too, lifted her off her feet and squeezed her tightly. Then he lowered his head to hers. She parted her lips to the welcome pressure of his tongue. He explored the cavern of her mouth as though savoring the flavor of her. Niccolo lifted his head and smiled down at her with a self-assurance that took her breath away. She could feel the heat surface in her cheeks, and was sure that her face was beet red.

Jagger cleared his throat loudly. "Umm, as lovely as this is, maybe we should move to the sitting room with the others." He shook his head, obviously not wanting to witness his parents' intimate reunion. "Besides, I'm not used to seeing my parents acting like a couple of teenagers."

165

Sasha's face was flaming hot now, while Niccolo let out a loud belly laugh. "Get used to it, son."

"Good grief." Jagger rolled his eyes before leaving the two alone in the hall.

"Niccolo, put me down." She pushed at his chest.

"Do I have to?"

"Yes."

"As Romeo would say, 'you're no damn fun.'"

"That is not what you said last night and this morning." She poked her tongue at him.

"You little minx. I should paddle you bottom for being such a tease."

"Is that a promise?"

"*Strega,*" he whispered as he set her on her feet. "I missed you."

"Did you really?" she asked in wonder.

"Of course, I did." By the tone of his voice and the look in his eyes, she could tell he was sincere.

"Niccolo, where do we go from here?"

"Short term or long term?"

"Both, I suppose."

"I know that I want you near me. I would like you to consider living with me in L.A. That's my home base, though I have other homes you may like better. As you know, things still are not quite safe for anyone associated with Dante and the rest of us, but my enemies are aware of you and Jagger, so there isn't much we can do about that now. Dante suggested that you and Jagger temporarily stay with my brother GianMarco and his wife Maggie. We have Underground agents who don't live far from there who watch their house.

Marco is also quite fierce and not one to be trifled with. He'll keep the two of you safe."

"Why can't we live with you?"

"You would be with me."

"Not if we're living with your brother!"

"It's only temporary, just until we figure a few things out."

"Like what?"

"Like finding out what your father's involvement is in this whole debacle."

"My father? What do you mean? What does he have to do with any of this?" Her father was many things and very secretive at times, but she didn't think even he would be so low as to harm his own grandson. How was it possible that he was involved?

"I can understand why you'd be confused. Things remain unclear, but over the course of the past few days, Jagger learned vital information. All I can say, Sasha, is that something big is going on. It is bigger than any of us could have imagined."

"How so?"

"It was one thing when we believed there was a rogue named *Il Diavolo*, who has aligned a number of minions for purposes unknown. We initially believed that he was simply killing other vampires for the power he could absorb. We then learned this particular rogue has a vendetta against our Grimaldi clan. Now we know that the vendetta is just a small part of his mission, and possibly *Il Diavolo* isn't the rogue we're looking for."

"Then what is it all about?" Sasha still had difficulty following him.

"I think I know why your father wanted Petra and me to be together. I want to confront him and see his reactions."

"Why? Tell me."

"I can't until I know for sure."

"I have a right to know."

Niccolo didn't look like he wanted to tell her anything more, but he must have read the determined expression on her face. He sighed. "There's been a movement taking place that involves all immortals. It's ..."

"What?"

"It's a movement to take out all humans."

"What? So you mean all those people? Did Jagger —"

"No. They tried to get him to participate, but he fought it. They finally turned on him because of it. Thank God he instinctively called out to me or he might be dead."

"Thank goodness for that. But why would they have taken him in the first place?"

"The head rogue was toying with him for his own purposes. He even pretended he was Jagger's father. There had to be magic involved — black magic."

"This is all very complicated. How do you think they would try to pull it off? There's only a few million immortals, there's billions of humans."

"There may not be as many immortals as there are humans, but think about it: a handful of determined immortals could take out a stadium full of people if they wanted to. Imagine what several thousand can do. This rogue has been slowly recruiting and building up his army over many years. Not even Dante knows how many are involved, but we've learned that the Council is a part of it. Your friend Yuri was also involved in this movement, as well as your father."

"Are you certain? Yuri, perhaps ... but my father? It's madness."

"You don't have to tell me that.." He took a deep breath and exhaled slowly. "Do you know what else is madness?"

"No. What?"

"Despite everything going on, I can't stop thinking about fucking you."

Her breath caught in her throat. She wanted it, too, but she wouldn't let him divert her. "You will not make me forget that you plan on leaving me behind again. If anyone should confront my father, it should be me. I'm going with you and you're not going to argue with me about it."

"I insist you go to my brother's. You and Jagger will be safe there."

"No. Haven't you learned from the past few days that despite your good intentions, we'll never be completely safe? Send Jagger to your brother but not me. I have to go. Don't you see? I need answers, too. You've had little interaction with my father, but I have had to deal with him most of my life. No, I'll go with you and if you refuse me, I'll find my own way there."

Niccolo sighed as though realizing he was fighting a losing battle.

"Fine, but I want you close to me at all times."

"Thank you!" She threw her arms around his neck and pressed her lips against his throat.

"Are you two going to stay in the hallway necking or are you going to join the rest of us?" Romeo stood at the end of the hall, looking at them with a smirk on his handsome face. In her opinion, he was very good-looking, but he was no Niccolo.

She had met both brothers around the same time and always wondered what would have happened if she had fallen for Romeo instead. He probably would have driven her crazy with his fast lifestyle, but she sensed there was a heart of gold under Romeo's rough-and-tumble exterior. It would take a special woman to tame his wild heart. Sasha was pleased because she knew she had the right brother.

Niccolo growled at his brother. "Can't a man get a little privacy with his woman?"

"Sheesh, not you, too!"

"What's that supposed to mean?"

"I guess this settling-down shit is contagious: first Marco, and now you. You two stay away from me. I don't want it rubbing off." Romeo made the sign of the cross before walking off.

Sasha giggled. "Your poor brother. When he finally finds his mate, he's going to fall hard."

"Yes, I think so, too. Come on, let's join the others." Niccolo held his hand out to her. She slipped her hand into his.

She loved this man so much.

Jagger was happy. It almost seemed as though the past few days had been only a bad dream. After cleaning up and resting, everyone decided to have one last meal together before they split up. He sat at the table between his parents. He couldn't stop looking over to his father. He had to keep pinching himself to assure he wasn't in a dream. His real father was actually here with him! In addition, two of his uncles sat across from them. They were also fascinating to watch, reminding him of his maternal uncles in their way.

They may have only had a few hours together but there was no doubt in Jagger's mind that his father truly loved him. The connection he felt with the much older man was strong, as it should be. He could feel the love in the way his father looked at him and in his tone. Every now and then his father would take his hand and squeeze it. For the first time in Jagger's life, he felt like he was whole. Jagger knew his mother wanted him to be a great warlock and realize his full potential, but among his father and paternal uncles, he felt like he was with his own kind. He was ready to embrace his vampire side.

It was unfortunate his first blood had been given under such stressful circumstances, but he'd discovered that he liked blood and wanted more. The way his father and uncles had taken out those rogues so brutally had awakened a part of him he hadn't known existed. It was violent, deadly, and hungry, and it wanted to be unleashed.

Jagger knew he could never completely let go of his warlock training because it was also a part of him, but now he knew which side he wanted to embrace the most. He glanced over at his Uncle Dante, head of the Underground, forceful and self-assured. Jagger admired his take-charge attitude. He had to remember to approach him later about offering his services to the Underground.

He turned to face his Uncle Romeo, whose fearlessness had taken Jagger's breath away. He knew there was another uncle he had yet to meet, but judging by his father and uncles Dante and Romeo, Jagger was sure he'd admire him just as much.

His mother leaned her head against his shoulder and he kissed her cheek. He regretted having worried her so much, but things had worked out for the best. His father took his hand again, but this time held on to it. Sitting here between his mother and father, he felt as though he had finally come home.

# Chapter Fifteen

Niccolo turned the shower to Cool. He was horny as hell and wanted some pussy—Sasha's pussy, to be exact. One taste wasn't enough. He knew he should probably let her rest because they had an early flight to Moscow, but this need within him would not go away.

The cool beads of water pounded against his heated skin, but it didn't douse the flames within. He cursed in frustration as he turned off the water and stepped out of the shower stall. It was good to finally be cleaned of all the rogue blood, and he felt refreshed, but he was ready to fuck now. After drying off, he sought out Sasha's room, not caring that he was nude.

He found her staring out her bedroom window, her arms wrapped around her body as though she were cold.

"Sasha," he whispered. She turned, almost as if she had anticipated his presence. Bathed by the light of the moon she looked luminous. Her cloak of sable hair draped around her body, and her dark brown eyes were wide and expectant.

"You've come, after all. What took you so long?" She looked straight at his cock.

"I talked with Jagger, then I showered. You knew I would be coming to you tonight?" His voice was full of amusement as he slowly walked to her.

"Yes, I knew. You seem insatiable of late, so it was clear it would be only a matter of time." She grabbed the hem of her lacy white nightgown and lifted the garment over her head.

Her small white breasts looked ready for the worship of his hands and mouth.

Sasha discarded her panties and flung them at him. Niccolo caught the underwear in his hand and brought it to his nose. "It smells delicious."

He tossed them aside. She shivered as he cupped her breasts in his palms. Niccolo leaned down and grazed her neck with his mouth. He squeezed and kneaded her taut mounds in his hands.

" Niccolo, that feels so good."

"And I intend to make you feel even better. I love the sensation of your skin under my hands and my mouth." He ran his tongue across her collarbone. Her skin tasted clean and fresh, titillating his taste buds. He knelt down in front of her, never letting go of her breasts. He tweaked the two hard nipples between his fingers, making Sasha wiggle her body against him. He could tell she was enjoying his touch as much as he was enjoying touching her. She felt so damn good.

Niccolo released one breast to trail a hand down the center of her body before letting it run across her hip to her ass. He kissed her flat belly, letting his tongue dip into her navel. He let his other hand fall to caress her stomach as he gripped her backside tightly.

"It's hard to believe that my son rested here. You're so small, so perfect," he whispered against her stomach.

She looked down at him, her dark eyes clouded with desire. It filled him with masculine pride that he was the cause of it. Everything about her turned him on—her petite but well-proportioned body, the way she looked at him when he touched her, the feel of her skin, and the tangy smell of her pussy.

Niccolo intended to savor every single inch of that wonderful-smelling cunt of hers. He was hungry and ready to eat. He grabbed her hips. "Open your legs, baby. I want some pussy."

Sasha planted her feet further apart, allowing him to stick his head between her legs. Niccolo nuzzled the soft pubic hair, reveling in the feel of it against his skin before inhaling her essence. The scent made him dizzy with desire for her. She ground her pussy against his face.

"Hold my shoulder tightly," he ordered softly as he lifted one of her legs over his shoulder. She complied. Niccolo inserted two fingers inside her damp channel. "Good, you're already wet for me. You want this, don't you, baby?"

"You know I do."

"Then tell me how much you want my mouth on your pussy."

"I want it badly. Don't torture me when I need you like this. I want it all, your fingers, mouth, and cock."

"I think that can be arranged." He smiled before using his free hand to part her slick folds. He dipped his head and licked her clit.

Sasha shook with obvious delight. "Oh, yes, yes, yes."

His tongue licked and stroked the hot little button before sucking it into his mouth. He felt her fingers dig into his shoulders. She moaned and sighed, but he sensed she was holding back. Niccolo wanted her to cry out his name, wanted her to show him how much she enjoyed what he was doing to her.

Niccolo began to move his fingers inside of her with slow, steady strokes. Sasha let out a moan. "Yes, just like that."

She moved her body up and down on his hand. His fingers were drenched in her juices as he thrust them into her more forcefully. "Scream for me, Sasha. I want to hear you call out my name."

"But everyone will hear."

"So what?"

"Our son —"

"I doubt our son is unfamiliar with this act. He's an adult. He'll know how much I desire his mama and how much she desires me. Let me hear you, sweetheart."

"Oh, Niccolo," she whispered.

He plunged his fingers into her, harder still. "Louder!"

"Niccolo!" she obeyed.

He added another finger inside of her hot, wet cunt, stretching her walls.

"Louder!" he demanded, twisting his fingers inside of her, allowing his fingers to shift and lengthen slightly, and delve deeper until she gave him the response he had been looking for.

She threw her head back and let out a loud scream. "Yes! Oh, God, Niccolo, fuck me with your fingers. Don't stop licking me, either." Her cream dripped liberally from her pussy.

He removed his cum-drenched fingers from inside her to lick them off, never taking his gaze off hers. She panted, her skin flushed and her pupils dilated from need. She looked exactly how he felt. Horny as hell, and he liked it.

Niccolo reached up and rubbed his fingers across her bottom lip. "Taste yourself." Her tongue snaked out to taste the juice he had smeared over her mouth. "Delicious, isn't it?"

Sasha nodded, unable to form the words to speak. Niccolo had magical hands. Why else would her body react so violently to his touch? The wild wanton passion running through her made her body shake and knees weak. Sasha gripped his shoulders tightly to steady herself. She didn't know how much longer she would be able to stand up against his skillful assault.

She watched in anticipation as his head dipped again and he ran his tongue along the inside of her thighs. She felt so hot, and her pussy was literally throbbing for him. The way he had fucked her with his fingers left her breathless and wanting more. His tongue slid to her labia, sucking them into his mouth. The pressure generated by the sucking sensation made her squirm.

Sasha moaned and couldn't stop. At first she was scared to cry out so loudly, afraid of what the others would think, but now the only thing she cared about was showing Niccolo how good his touch felt and how badly she wanted him. She looked down at his dark head between her thighs. His mouth latched on to the opening of her damp pussy, and she was delirious with lust.

He slurped and licked at her pussy like a starving man. She realized he was feeding off of her juices. There was nothing more erotic than a sexy vampire feasting voraciously on one's cunt. Shivers of rapture and delight coursed through her.

"Oh, God. Eat it! That's right," she moaned.

Niccolo sucked on her pussy until a strong vibration rocked her body, taking her to a peak so intense she felt her body seize up. "Oh, God, I can't take anymore!" Her knees felt weak; she didn't think they were strong enough to support her any longer.

As though he had read her mind, Niccolo grabbed her hips and held her steady while he continued to lick, suck, and feast on her pussy. His mouth on her was like pure magic; she succumbed to the pleasure, never wanting the moment to end. The way he ate her pussy made her so delirious she felt like crying from the sheer joy of the moment. Sasha had never thought it was possible to feel this good or that she could be taken to such a torrid peak. By the time he lifted his head and pushed her leg down from his shoulder, she was numb from pleasure.

Niccolo stood up, towering over her. His amber eyes glowed with lust, filling her with excitement. She was woman enough to know that he was far from finished with her. But she was surprised when he lifted her off her feet and, instead of carrying her over to the king-sized bed that sat in the middle of the room, he pushed her up against the wall, and propelled his cock into her wet hole.

Although they'd fucked before, she was still amazed at the sheer size of him, and the delectable sensation of his penis filling her so wonderfully.

"You are so tight around my cock. I've wanted to do this to you all day," he murmured, burying his face into her neck.

"I've wanted you inside of me all day," she whispered back.

"Wrap your legs around my waist."

She did as he commanded and draped her arms around his neck, surrendering to the sizzling passion of their lovemaking. Sasha tightened her pussy muscles around his cock, reveling at the way he plowed in and out of her.

"Yes! Give it to me! Harder! Faster!" she demanded passionately. Her body felt as though it were melting with need for him. Sasha couldn't get enough of his exquisite cock. He thrust deeper and deeper into her until she didn't think he could go any further. She felt one with him. He satisfied the desire in her heart and the ache in her pussy.

"Like silk," he whispered against her skin, and pressed kisses to her throat. His warm breath against her flesh sent tingles up and down her spine. She could feel another explosive orgasm erupting through her body and clung to him tightly.

"*Belissima*, I want more. I want to be inside all of your holes."

Her head shot up as he slid his sopping wet cock out of her cunt. She tensed up as it poked insistently at her virgin asshole. "Niccolo, I --"

"Shh, it's okay, *belissima*. If you don't like it, I promise to stop. My cock is so slick from your cream I'll have no problem sliding into that tight little bud. Just say the word and I won't do it." He kissed her neck.

"But you're so large. My pussy is one thing, but ..."

"You will be surprised at what your body can take. You were made for me. Please give me your ass," he coaxed, kissing her as he nibbled on her neck. She didn't think she would enjoy it, but she wanted very much to please him, and she *was* curious to know what it would feel like to have her ass fucked. She trusted that he would stop if she asked him to.

She nodded silently. He gathered some more of her cream and smeared it around and just inside the tight ring of her anus, then pressed the tip of his cock against the opening.

"It may hurt a little in the beginning, but you need to relax, okay?"

"Yes," she whispered.

Sasha squeezed her eyes tightly closed as the head of his dick slipped inside her ass. Holy shit, it hurt! She bit down on her lip hard so that she wouldn't scream out.

"It's okay, baby. It's okay." He soothed her. "Do you want me to take it out?"

She gritted her teeth. "No." With each passing second, she relaxed a little more. He slid deeper into her. Sasha let out a loud gasp.

"That's it, baby. Relax. Take my cock within you," he urged.

Her breathing evened out, and the pain slowly faded until it was gone. It wasn't as bad as she'd thought it would be. Actually, as Niccolo began to gently pump into her, it felt rather nice. A slow warmth built inside the pit of her stomach.

"Do you like it, baby? Do you like the feel of my cock inside your tight little ass?"

"Yes," she moaned, leaning her head against the wall.

"Good, because I like fucking your ass almost as much as I enjoy fucking your pussy. They both belong to me. You belong to me -- every single delectable inch of you."

His words filled her with happiness.

"I want you to tell me who your pussy belongs to."

"You."

"This ass?"

"You."

"Your body?"

"You."

His amber eyes looked deeply into hers. "It works both ways you know. I belong to you, too."

"Yes." A tear slid down her cheek. She couldn't remember ever being this happy. He leaned over and kissed the trail her tear had made. With one more hard thrust, she felt his seed explode into her ass, triggering another mind-blowing climax within her.

When Niccolo slid out of her, she felt empty. He carried her to the shower where he pushed her under the cool spray of the water. They soaped each other, and Sasha took special care with his cock. She wanted him again. As though he had read her mind, she found herself pressed against the shower stall with his cock planted firmly in her well-used pussy. Niccolo fucked her hard and fast. She clung to him helplessly, delighting in the exquisite pleasure of the moment.

Her knees would not support her when Niccolo eased his cock out of her this time. Once he finished drying her off, he carried her to the bed and laid her down, stretching out next to her. He gave her one last lingering kiss on her lips before clicking off the lamp beside the nightstand.

"That was wonderful, *belissima*." He pulled her into his arms.

"Mmm." She was too content to speak.

"I don't know what it is, but whenever I hold you, kiss you ... I need you more. I still feel a struggle inside, but it lessens each time we're together like this. This time I know for certain I can never let you go."

"I don't want you to let me go, Niccolo. I love you so much. I don't know when you'll be able to say those words to me, but I want you to know how I feel."

She saw his eyes glow and wondered what he was thinking.

"I don't know if I really know what love is. If it's thinking about you every second of the day when I know my mind should be on other things, or having my body ache from wanting you so much, or wanting to keep you safe, and needing you next to me always, then I must be in love with you. Now, let's get some sleep, *strega mia*, before I'm tempted to fuck you again."

Sasha knew that tomorrow would be a trying day for the both of them, but all she could think about was how happy and in love she was.

## Chapter Sixteen

Romeo nudged him. "Cheer up, kiddo, everything will be okay."

Jagger stared out the window of his uncle's pickup. "I'm not a child. I can understand my mother's feelings. I will always be her baby, regardless of what age I am, but I'm disappointed my father would allow Uncle Dante to send me off as if I couldn't handle myself."

"You have to remember how close we came to losing you. I think a little experience would do you some good, but it's not my call. Hey, I'd rather be with them, too, but what big brother says goes." Romeo shrugged.

"Do you always listen to him?" Jagger lifted a brow, still trying to figure out the Grimaldi family dynamics.

"He's the only one I'll take orders from. Sometimes he's more like a father than he is a brother. I'm not one to take orders well, but for him, I'd take the proverbial stake through the heart."

"You must be very close to him."

"Yes." The older vampire didn't elaborate. They drove in silence on their way to his Uncle GianMarco's house. Jagger was still a little upset about not being able to go with his parents to face his grandfather. This involved him as much as it did the others. Hadn't he been the one able to collect valuable information?

Now that he had tasted first blood, Jagger felt stronger than ever. His confidence level had risen and he believed he could take out any rogue who crossed his path. Perhaps when his mother, father, and Uncle Dante returned from Russia he could point out his usefulness to their cause. Eventually they would realize that he could hold his own. For now, it was frustrating to be so far away, unable to do anything to help.

Romeo began to chuckle.

Jagger looked over. "What are you laughing at?"

"You. Your thoughts amuse me."

Jagger glared at him. "I didn't give you permission to read my mind."

"Yes, you did. You give any vampire the right to read your mind if you don't close it. In human years, you would be considered mature and capable of making such decisions, but we live forever, and you still have a lot to learn. That is why your father didn't want you to go with him. He has your best interests at heart."

"I'm tired of being treated like I'm a child. I managed to kill a rogue when it was six against one. I'd be able to hold my own in any fight." Jagger pounded his fist into his hand.

"I know, but in time, you'll see plenty of action. You're just not ready for Underground business yet."

"I have a right to be involved. Aren't I a Grimaldi? I have the added edge of powers beyond that of a normal vampire. My training is nearly complete. When my Uncle Blade comes back from his sojourn, I'll be finished in no time."

"Your powers will prove very valuable — one day."

"But —"

"No buts."

Jagger rolled his eyes before looking out the window again, the frustration nearly choking him.

"Your thoughts are showing again. You're really worried about your parents, aren't you?'

"How can I not be? My mother shouldn't have gone—she has no powers at all and my father ... well, I just found him."

"And you don't want to lose him? It's understandable. I worry about my brothers with each and every mission, as I'm sure they worry about me. That's what families do."

"I'm looking forward to getting to know all of my father's family. What's my Uncle GianMarco like?"

"You'll like him very much. He's got an artistic soul, so don't be surprised if he asks you to sit for him. He's managed to rope even me into sitting for him a few times. They were the most boring hours of my life, but the end result was amazing. His stuff is like nothing anyone has seen before." Jagger could hear the pride in Romeo's voice and smiled.

"What else can you tell me about him?"

"He can be quite outspoken. I think you'll also like his wife. Maggie's a lovely woman. They're expecting their first child together in a few months, although she has two adult children already. I warn you though, you should probably have a barf bag available. The way those two carry on, you'd think no one had ever been in love before."

"You sound like you don't approve."

"It's not that I don't approve. I'm happy for them. That kind of life just isn't for me."

"Why not? Isn't it everyone's desire to find their true mate?"

"Not mine. The responsibility would get on my nerves. Look, there's the house." Romeo pointed to a large estate situated on several acres of land. The big white house was not quite a mansion, but it was still quite large. Romeo pulled into the driveway and drove a little further to park.

"Here we are, kiddo, your safe haven for the next few days."

The front door flew open. A tall man with shoulder-length blond hair and dark brows walked toward them. As he got closer, Jagger noticed the man's amber-colored eyes. This had to be his uncle.

"Jagger! At last!" The older vampire came forward and pulled Jagger into his arms. Jagger automatically returned the hug as though it were the most natural thing in the world.

The smile his uncle bestowed upon him was sincere and he felt welcomed. "My wife has been cooking like a demon since we found out you were on your way. I hope you're hungry because while you're here, you'll get fed plenty. If it were not for our naturally high metabolism I would have gained a ton of weight by now from all of her good cooking. Come inside, we have other company. My stepdaughter surprised us with a visit." GianMarco turned to his brother.

"Hey, Ro, I see you're still in one piece. What are you being punished for this time?" GianMarco whispered *sotto voce* to Jagger. "Usually when Dante takes him away from the action, he's done something bad."

"Don't be such a brat, Marco. I've done nothing. Dante felt the mission they were on required a little more diplomacy than I was willing to exert," Romeo muttered, sounding annoyed.

"I see." GianMarco smiled, amusement gleaming in his eyes.

Jagger liked the lighthearted exchange between the two brothers. He was almost envious of their closeness.

"Come on, guys." GianMarco led them into the house. The minute Jagger stepped though the front door, the smell of good old-fashioned American cooking hit him. Even though the house was large, it still had a homey feeling.

"This is a nice place," Jagger said politely.

"Thanks. It's mostly Maggie's doing ... well, she tells me what to do and I do it." GianMarco chuckled.

"You're whipped," Romeo said with disgust.

"Jealous?" GianMarco retorted, seemingly unbothered by his brother's taunt. Just by the way he spoke her name, it was clear to Jagger that GianMarco was deeply in love with his wife.

A pretty African-American woman came into the room to greet them. She was positively glowing with a radiant smile on her face and a twinkle in her eyes. This must be *the* Maggie Jagger had already heard so much about. She walked up to Romeo and gave him a hug.

"It's good to see you in one piece," she teased, echoing her husband's earlier words.

Romeo brushed his lips against her check. "It's good to see you're getting better at walking bowlegged. That baby is going to have a bone to pick with the two of you when it finally gets here," he shot back.

Maggie giggled, smacking him playfully against the arm before turning to Jagger and giving him a warm smile. "So you're Niccolo's son. Welcome to the family." She hugged him.

Jagger couldn't help but to return her embrace; her curvaceous frame exuded warmth. It was little wonder his Uncle GianMarco was so smitten with her. Jagger decided he liked her very much.

"You look just like your father. The resemblance is startling. What should I call you? Do you prefer Jagger or Nikolai?"

"I'll answer to either one, but not very many people call me by my first name, so Jagger is fine."

"That's an interesting name, Jagger. How did your mother come up with it?" Maggie asked.

"It's a tradition in my mother's family, passed down from her mother's side, to name their male children based on their special gifts. The males in my family can manipulate metal and cut any type of metal surface. For example, my three maternal uncles all have traditional Russian first names, but they're also known by their second names like me. My mother couldn't think of a middle name for me at first, but when I was a couple of days old, my Uncle Blade dangled a metal rattle in front of me, which I somehow splintered into jagged little pieces. She didn't want to call me Splinter, so she settled for Jagger; hence, my name."

"That's very interesting." Maggie smiled. "Well, I hope you're hungry. Camryn and I have been slaving in the kitchen."

"Camryn?"

"My daughter. She's still in the kitchen. I'll go get her." Maggie turned around, then stopped. "Oh, here she is."

From the corner of his eye, Jagger caught the shape of a feminine figure walking slowly toward them. He turned to see the newcomer and froze. There was no mistaking the relationship between mother and daughter. They looked a lot alike but different. The younger version was an absolute vision.

His mouth went dry.

Camryn was around the same height as her mother, but where her mother was voluptuous, she was slender, yet rounded in all the right places, especially her rear. Big brown eyes were set in a beautiful milk chocolate face. Her hair was pulled back into a big bushy ponytail. She looked young, but she had to be at least eighteen or nineteen.

"Camryn, this is Jagger, GianMarco's nephew, and you already know Romeo."

Jagger barely registered the hand Camryn offered in welcome. She was so beautiful. He couldn't move to save his life. If he touched her, he wasn't sure if he would be able to let go. Where the hell had she been all his life?

An awkward silence fell in the room. Maggie frowned and shot her husband a questioning look. Jagger realized how rude his behavior appeared, but he feared he would do something stupid if he moved. Camryn dropped her hand, looking slightly offended. "Umm, Nice to meet you, Jagger. I guess I'll go to check on the food." She turned around abruptly and went back toward the kitchen.

"And I need to drain the lizard," Romeo announced unnecessarily. He whistled as he strode out the room and headed to what Jagger assumer was the lavatory. That left him alone with Maggie and GianMarco, who stared at him with concern in their eyes.

"Are you okay, Jagger? Do you need to rest?" his uncle asked.

"Umm, no, I'm fine. That was very rude of me. I meant no offense."

Maggie didn't say anything. She actually looked ill. "Are you all right?" Jagger asked her.

"Maggie is still suffering nausea from the pregnancy."

"Yes, I think I need to go the bathroom as well. Make yourself at home, Jagger." She spun around.

"I'm going to go with her. Will you be okay by yourself?"

"Yes, go ahead."

Left alone, Jagger found himself wandering to the kitchen. Camryn was bent over, taking a dish out of the oven. The sight of her plump rear made his cock stir. The scent of her perfume filled his nostrils as he stepped closer. She was magnificent. He had never met a woman he had felt such an instant connection to.

187

Camryn straightened up as if she sensed she was no longer alone. Slowly turning to face him, she gave him a wary look. "Yes?"

"That smells delicious," he said, stepping closer.

"Oh, yeah, my mom's peach cobbler is the best. I'm sure you'll like it."

He wasn't about to correct her by saying he had been referring to her pussy and not the cobbler. When he didn't say anything, she took a step back. "Why are you staring at me like that? Don't they have black people where you come from?"

"Plenty, but that's not why I'm staring at you."

"Well, whatever your reason, didn't your mother ever teach you that it's rude to stare?"

"I'm sure she did but I can't help it. I ... you're very beautiful."

She seemed surprised by his answer. "Umm, thanks."

"I apologize for my rudeness out there. I was stunned."

"By what?"

"By your beauty. Will you be here long? Perhaps we could go out for dinner sometime."

"I don't think so." She looked like she would rather be anywhere but standing there with him, but that didn't deter him.

"Why not? I will be visiting for a while and since you are here, perhaps—"

"I said no. Look, I'll be honest with you. I'm very happy my mother has found love again, but the bottom line is, he's a vampire. I didn't even believe in them until a few months ago. You're my stepfather's nephew, so you're obviously one of them."

188

"So? What's wrong with that?"

"I'm not saying anything is wrong, but I'd prefer a human male. No offense."

"I don't see how I'm supposed to not take offense. Your mother seems so warm and open-minded. I didn't think her daughter would be otherwise." He surveyed the kitchen until they rested on a box of aluminum foil. Jagger used his hand to guide the box into the air, opening it to allow a long sheet of foil to break off.

He heard her gasp, but concentrated on his task. He directed the box back down on the counter while manipulating the sheet of foil. Jagger fashioned it into the shape of a rose. The foil rose moved through the air, stopping when it was in front of Camryn. She looked at him with wide eyes and didn't seem to want to touch it.

"Go ahead. Take it," he urged.

She hesitantly reached out to touch the metallic rose. "How did you do that?"

"I'm also a warlock. I'm not ashamed of what I am."

"As interesting as this is, why are you telling me this?"

"Because you intrigue me, and I'd like to get to know you better."

"I intrigue you? I don't know you from Adam. Maybe weak pick-up lines work well where you're from but they don't with me."

"So tell me what you want me to say and I'll say the words."

"I don't want you to say anything to me. You're coming on way too strong. Look, I'll pretend this never happened and you stay out of my way and I'll stay out of yours. How about that?"

She was feisty. Instead of it turning him off, it excited him. Getting feminine attention had always been easy for him. When he was fifteen, a sexy older woman had seduced him, and from then on, there was no holding back. He loved women—short, tall, thin, or plump. He loved everything about them. He loved their scents and he loved to eat pussy. In his short lifetime he had probably been with hundreds of women, but here was one who didn't seem affected by his looks or charm. Actually, she looked at him with a hint of dislike. It turned him on.

"Perhaps you can pretend, but I won't. What is it you have against vampires?"

"I have nothing against vampires. I just prefer human men."

"Have you ever been with a vampire?"

"No, but I don't have to taste poison to know it's bad for me."

"Apples and oranges, my dear. As I said before, you intrigue me."

"And you annoy me," she shot back, attempting to move past him.

He grasped her hand. "There's something you should know about me."

"There's nothing I want to know about you." She flashed angry brown eyes at him.

"Nonetheless, I will tell you. Besides being a hybrid vampire-warlock, I'm also very persistent. I've learned how detrimental it is when one of my kind has been denied what he wants and I won't deny myself now. Be warned, Camryn, because whether you wish to hear it or not—I want you."

## Chapter Seventeen

"This is it." Niccolo looked at Sasha, squeezing her hand. There was apprehension in her dark eyes. He could understand how she felt.

"Yes, this is it," she replied with an uneasy smile.

"Are you nervous?"

"Can't you tell? I'm practically shaking in my shoes."

"There's no time for nerves now. Let's go," Dante said, getting out of the car first.

Niccolo laughed humorlessly. "That brother of mine has nerves of steel. Sometimes his single-mindedness can be a little annoying."

"He's just very determined. It's understandable. You were the one who told me how he's dedicated his life to this cause, so he takes it very seriously." Sasha rubbed his arm.

"Yes, I suppose you're right. I still don't feel comfortable having you here with us. I wish you had gone with Jagger."

"And I already said I wouldn't allow you to leave me behind, so deal with it." Sasha looked at him defiantly.

Beneath her brave façade he could still sense her fear, and wished he could take her into his arms and rid her of it. "Stay close to me when we go in."

"Yes, I already know the drill," she answered before they got out of the car and walked to the front door. "I can't believe

I'm here so soon after telling my father I would never step foot in this house again." Sasha bit her lip.

"Yes, but when you said it, you meant it. Circumstances have changed."

Dante rang the doorbell.

An anxious anticipation Niccolo had not felt in a long time coursed through him. He felt almost as nervous as Sasha looked. There was no answer. Dante rang the bell again.

Still no answer.

Sasha frowned. "That's odd; usually Dmitri answers the door before someone even rings. I wonder what's going on." She reached forward to try the doorknob. She knew only family members could enter through the magical barrier surrounding the door unless they were specifically invited in. "It's locked, and the wards seem to be in place. I'll need one of you to kick the door in while my hand is on the door."

"I'm on it," Niccolo said. With one swift kick to the door, he sent it flying open. The moment he walked over the threshold, the feeling of danger made the hair on the back of his neck stand on end. Niccolo grabbed Sasha, pushing her behind him. He should have known to be on his guard the moment he'd stepped onto the warlock's property. Despite Sasha's words, he should have remembered the house was warded to protect its inhabitants; no wonder they hadn't immediately felt the danger.

"Something is going on within these walls," Dante said aloud exactly what he had been thinking.

The two vampires walked ahead while Sasha followed closely behind.

"I won't let you do this to me. I made you what you are!" they heard a voice yell from the back of the house.

"My father's study. Hurry!"

The men followed the sound of the yelling. Niccolo pushed open the door of the study and was immediately knocked back by a burst of light. He crashed into the opposite wall. Dante ran inside, and Niccolo sprang back to his feet. Racing into the study, he saw Ivan Romanov trying to fend off two rogue vampires and another warlock.

"What's going on in here?" Dante demanded. The rogues who were pummeling Ivan into a pulp stopped what they were doing and turned around. The unknown warlock shot them an angry glare.

"Leave now or you'll be next."

"Papa!" Sasha ran into the room, but Niccolo stopped her.

"No. Go back," he hissed at her.

"Yes, Sasha, leave. You also should take your own advice, vampire," the warlock taunted.

Niccolo's eyes narrowed. He had called Sasha by name, and she seemed to recognize him. Who was he?

"From what I see, it's three on one. How about letting us even up the odds?" Dante asked, letting his hands shift into claws. His eyes gleamed dangerously as he took a step toward the warlock, who seemed slightly intimidated by a vampire who was evidently not afraid of him.

"Who are you?" the warlock demanded.

"Dante Grimaldi, and you?"

"*The* Dante Grimaldi?" the warlock asked in obvious disbelief.

"At your service." Dante gave him a mock bow.

"And I suppose this is one of your brothers. I hear you don't go anywhere without them," the warlock sneered.

He introduced himself. "Niccolo Grimaldi. How about telling us what's going on before we kill you?"

"Yes, you are definitely a Grimaldi. You are both just as arrogant as I've heard. No matter, we came to take care of one little problem. I don't see why we can't kill two or three birds with one stone. Get them!" the warlock shouted.

The two rogues raced toward them. The larger of the two charged at Dante, while the smaller, stocky one tackled Niccolo, nearly sending him to the ground.

"Run, Sasha!" Niccolo shouted before a fist connected with his jaw. The blow sent him backward but he remained on his feet. He ducked another punch and delivered his own blow into the rogue's solar plexus.

To his surprise, he caught a glimpse of Sasha confronting the warlock. "Get the hell out of here, Sasha!" Stubborn woman, she was going to get herself killed! Why didn't she listen to what he told her? The rogue wrapped his fingers around Niccolo's throat.

Shit! Now he had to worry about her and staying alive, too.


"Why have you done this to my father, Leo?" Sasha asked the warlock. Leo Federov was one of her father's henchmen.

"You're not in a position to ask questions, Sasha."

"Don't give me that. Why would you do this to him? My father trusted you."

"Such familial loyalty from the discarded daughter. You should enjoy seeing us crush him." Leo sneered down at her father's bloodied, battered body. Ivan looked as though he was barely hanging on to life. "Run away now, Sasha, and I will spare you. Our grievance is not with you."

"Your grievance is most certainly with me. You've attacked my father and now the man I love."

"Fine. I had not planned to, but I will kill you, too. Say your goodbyes to your father now."

Sasha refused to let her father's whipping boy intimidate her. She had to think on her feet. Niccolo and Dante were battling the rogues; she knew she would have to act fast for their sakes as well as her father's and her own. She lowered herself to her knees, her mouth at her father's ear.

"Papa," she whispered tentatively, touching his bloody face. One lid slowly slid open to reveal a pain-filled blue eye. The life seemed to drain out of him with each passing second.

"Sasha ... you came to me."

"I will try to save you. You know what you must do." She whispered so Leo wouldn't hear. "Unbind me."

"No ... I can't let you face him. You're not strong enough. He'll kill you."

"He'll kill me anyway. At least I will be able to better defend myself. If I don't do something, we will all die. Papa, please."

For a moment he didn't respond and she feared he wouldn't as his breathing grew more ragged.

"Please, time is running out," she pleaded.

"*Arocko julium rigous mokton rushi ma balik wi. Wi balik ma rushi mokton rigous julium arocko,*" he murmured, then slumped back.

Leo reached down and grabbed a handful of her hair, pulling her up to her feet. "Time's up, Sasha. You could have been spared, but you wanted to be stubborn. So be it." Leo brought his hand up.

"No!" Across the room, Niccolo lifted his rogue up in the air and tossed him into a bookshelf before dashing over to them, and punched Leo on the side of the head.

195

The warlock had not seen it coming and loosened his grip on Sasha.

"Sasha, get the hell out of here before I toss your ass out myself!" Niccolo shouted.

"Niccolo, watch out!" The rogue he had been battling only seconds earlier charged toward him. Instinctively her hands shot out. To her surprise a bolt of power blasted from her fingers, knocking back the rogue clear across the room.

The charge from her body was so powerful, she also fell backward. Niccolo looked at her as though she had grown two heads. "I thought—"

"Think later, take him out now," she cut him off and returned her attention to Leo, who was slowly getting back to his feet.

"Ah, you want to challenge me." Leo laughed. "You're way out of your league, Sasha."

"Am I?" She held up the palm of her hand to show him her birthmark.

Leo looked astonished. "The mark of Hecate?"

"Yes."

He regained his composure almost immediately as though the mark was of no concern to him. "No matter, little Sasha. You don't know how to properly use it. At least I now know why your father never wanted to train you properly."

What was he talking about? He must have seen the look of confusion on her face.

"Oh? You didn't know? Well, I guess you'll never know now, because you're both going to die today."

Leo threw a ball of fire at her head. Thinking quickly, she puckered her lips and blew out a stream of air, freezing the ball's motion. The ice ball dropped to the floor, shattering into several pieces.

"Not bad. How about this?" Leo threw his fist out, sending an invisible punch to her stomach. The air slammed out of her body, making her double over.

*Concentrate, Sasha. You are rusty, but you have to do this,* she chanted to herself.

Another invisible fist hit her in the chest. She staggered, but she refused to fall. She threw two fists at the overconfident warlock, sending him flat on his ass.

"You little bitch. I was only toying with you before. Now I'm going to make sure it hurts when I kill you."

"Not if I kill you first." She prayed for the strength to pull this off. Sasha lifted her hands in the air. The room began to shake.

"What are you doing, you crazy bitch?" Leo was clearly stunned by the show of strength.

A book from a shelf flew at the warlock's head, followed by another, then another. Leo ducked, but the barrage of items that began to fly off the bookshelves was too much for him to fend off. He tried to redirect the flying objects in her direction, but suddenly things began to fly from all directions.

A heavy marble paperweight, which had rested on her father's desk, flew at Leo's head. This time the warlock didn't duck fast enough. It caught him on the side of the face, cutting his cheek wide open. He grabbed at the wound, not seeing the sharp letter opener flying his way. It flew with such force right through his ear that it came out the other side.

Leo clutched his head, then collapsed, dead before he hit the floor. Sasha lowered her arms, stunned at what she had done. She swiftly went to her father's side, holding his hand before lowering it. Her father had given her his remaining strength. It was the only reason she had been able to generate so much power after not having used her skills in so long.

She glanced at Niccolo and Dante, breathing a sigh of relief to see they had taken care of the two rogues, whose lifeless bodies now lay at their feet.

Niccolo rushed over to her. "Sasha, are you okay?"

He grabbed her, squeezing her against him as though he would absorb her into him. Then he held her away from him and started to shake her. "What the hell got into you? You could have been killed, dammit! I told you to run!"

"I wasn't going to leave you or my father."

"So you preferred sticking your neck on the line?! You nut! I ought to take you across my knee and spank you until you can't sit for weeks. If you ever pull a stunt like that again, that's exactly what I'm going to do! Do you understand me?"

She realized there was no point in arguing with him when he was like this; nonetheless, it was good to know he cared. "Yes, Niccolo," she said, mustering as much contriteness in her voice as she could.

A loud groan came from the floor. "Papa!" She twisted out of Niccolo's arms and went to her father's side. She would never have thought her strong-as-steel father could look like this. Tears sprang to her eyes as she gathered him into her arms, rocking him back and forth.

"*Devochka moya*. My little girl," he whispered.

"Papa?" He had never used that endearment with her before.

"I'm sorry for what I've done to you. You came to me despite—" he broke off as he coughed, spitting up a disturbing amount of blood.

"Please save your strength," she begged. "I'll try to heal you. I'm a bit rusty but—"

"No, my little one. I must pay a penance for my sins. There is no second chances for me. My time is not long for this world. I have been a foolish old man." He coughed again.

She saw Niccolo and Dante hovering over them. She shook her head at them. Seeming to understand, they backed away but did not leave the room.

"You must rest." Sasha stroked her father's face.

"No. I know you need answers and you deserve them. Listen to me. You have to understand what's going on." He paused for a moment as if he was trying to figure out where to begin. "I have wronged you and all because I was jealous ... jealous of that mark on your hand. The mark of Hecate is only granted to a few witches in a millennium, and you are one of the chosen ones. I told myself it should have been me. I slighted you in your training and belittled you when you made a mistake so you would lose your confidence. So help me, I knew what I did was wrong, but I just couldn't stop myself. Even though you won't believe me, I do care for you, Sasha. You were my baby. It was just so much easier to get along with your brothers because they are male, and your sister, God rest her soul, was so like me, and compliant to my wishes ... well, that's no excuse, and I'm more sorry than you can imagine for everything I've done."

Tears ran down her face. He did love her. Finally, the acceptance and acknowledgment she had been waiting for her entire life, but the words were bittersweet because her father barely clung to life.

"Please say you forgive me, Sasha. I can die in peace if I know I have your forgiveness."

"You hurt me very badly, but you are my father, and because of that I forgive you."

"You have a kind heart; it is more than I deserve. Now, listen carefully, because this is important ... it concerns you all."

Immediately, Niccolo and Dante stepped forward and knelt next to the dying warlock.

"I must apologize to you, Niccolo. I used you for my own means. I knew you didn't realize you were falling for Sasha, just as she already had for you, but it didn't fit my plans for you two to be together, so I cast a spell that you would fall for Petra instead. The spell was twofold: while you loved Petra, you would feel the opposite for Sasha. In my jealousy for my own child, I sought to punish her through you. But I see you have managed to overcome the spell. No matter how strong the enchantment spell is, it can't trump the bond of true mates, or in your case Niccolo, bloodmates. I'm happy to see this."

"Why? Why did you cause your own daughter so much heartache? Because of you, I missed the most important years of my son's life. Maybe Sasha is ready to forgive you, but I am not," Niccolo hissed at her father. His eyes glowed with anger.

"Please, Niccolo, he's dying," Sasha pleaded.

"After what he did to you? To us? He deserves to burn in hell!"

"Hear him out, Nico." Dante touched Niccolo on the shoulder in a gesture of comfort.

Niccolo pursed his lips mutinously, but didn't speak.

Sasha turned back to her father.

"I don't blame you. If I were in your shoes, I don't know how forgiving I would be either. In any event, the Council is planning to make a move toward world domination. They're slowly killing off groups of humans associated with any immortal. The message being sent is to join them or be destroyed. There's been talk for years of breeding a super immortal ... I thought who would make a better mix than a Romanov and a Grimaldi. Petra was devoted to the cause and was willing to bear a half vampire child. I..." he broke off coughing, spitting out more blood. After a moment, he continued, visibly weaker.

"Thirty years ago, I sent out a message to someone I knew was connected to your Underground on a pretext to get one of the Grimaldis here. I thought with our two families merged, we would be unstoppable, but Romeo wouldn't stay in one place long enough to really pay much attention to Petra, and you, Niccolo, though you were charmed by her beauty, there was no spark between you two. Sasha was kept ignorant about the movement because it didn't suit me at the time to bring her into my confidence. I saw the secret looks you and Sasha exchanged. Still, I would not be thwarted in my plans, so I cast the spell on you. You were putty in Petra's hands afterwards, but then *he* found out and ... they tore her to pieces."

A tear slid from his pale blue eye.

"In my hurt and anger, I lashed out at Sasha. I bound her powers because I convinced myself that she was the root of all my problems. It was that damn mark again. The old jealousy resurfaced, and, once again, I let my little girl down and bound her powers. But by that time, I was in too deep. They had killed Petra, but I thirsted for power and vengeance. I moved to take control from *him*, and lost my sons because they wanted nothing more to do with me. My wife has left me, and even those I trusted have turned on me. After what they did to Jagger, I spoke out against *him*. I tried to get out but ... he can't be stopped. The Council. They're all in on it. They're being controlled by him."

"Who are you talking about? What is his name?" Dante asked.

"*Il Demonio* he calls himself, but his name is Adonis."

The collective gasps of the two vampires made Sasha's heat shoot up. What was the significance of that name?

"Who is he to us?" Dante asked.

"Don't you know? He's your brother," the warlock said, his voice slowly fading with each word.

"Then who the hell is *il Diavolo?*" Dante would not let up.

201

"Also your brother." Ivan closed his eyes for the last time.

## Chapter Eighteen

"Are you okay, Niccolo?" Sasha wrapped her arms around his waist and rested her head against his chest. He didn't really know how to answer her. For the first time in a long time, he felt like himself again. Things seemed right and he was with the woman of his heart.

His bloodmate.

He loved her and he was free to feel this way without the cloud of the spell hovering over him. One part of him was happier than he could imagine, but another part of him was worried and frightened about what was to come. Ivan's last words didn't answer all of their questions; in fact, they had only generated more. Were *il Demonio* and *il Diavolo* in fact two different rogues, and how was it possible that he or they could be their brothers? There were no other brothers he knew of unless ... was their papa still alive?

No. He couldn't be. Dante was absolutely sure he had witnessed their papa's death. Not only that, Dante had said the redheaded rogue in Salzburg mentioned the name Giovanni. What did it mean? Their papa's name had been Giovanni, too. None of this made sense. At least they knew the Council's plans now. Niccolo figured Dante knew even more beyond that. His brother had looked pale at the warlock's last words.

He hadn't said much on the plane trip home, and the moment they'd stepped off the plane, Dante had said he needed to go home and take care of a few things. They would meet at GianMarco's the next day.

203

Niccolo didn't want to go to his brother's right away. He wanted to have Sasha to himself for the night; he knew more trouble would ensue within the next few days.

"I'm fine," he finally answered.

"Your lips say you're fine, but your eyes tell a different story. We are one now, and you should be able to tell me anything," she said, rubbing her head beneath his chin.

"I fear something big is going to happen."

"You mean what the Council is planning?"

"Yes. Can you imagine the chaos? Where would it end? They plan on taking out humans. Let's say their plan is successful. What would they do next? Do you think they would be satisfied with just humans? What if they decided to take out immortals that didn't fit their mold? Their idea to breed a super immortal worries me. Who says that once there are enough of them that they don't try to wipe the rest of us out? Even if they don't intend to get rid of us, they would try to control us. We can't let them win."

"And we won't."

"I wish I had your confidence right now."

"I'm confident because I have faith in you."

"It doesn't bother you that my brother will need me?"

"No, because I plan on being by your side through this entire thing. Jagger has already expressed an interest in joining the Underground."

"Absolutely not on both counts. I can't risk losing either one of you."

"I can't say I'm crazy about the idea of Jagger joining either, but he has that trademark Grimaldi stubbornness. One thing I've realized after nearly losing him is that Jagger is a man, not a little boy, and he has to make his own decisions. If that decision includes joining the Underground, then so be it."

"Dante would never allow it. He's too young."

"Says who?"

"Says me, and my brother will think so as well."

"I'm sure Jagger will have plenty to say about that, but I'll allow him to fight his own battles, and what a battle it will be when you forbid him to join." She smiled mischievously. "While we're on the subject, why can't I help? I'm older. I have my powers back and they're stronger than ever."

"Yes, but you're my woman and you haven't trained in a very long time. You shouldn't involve yourself in this."

"What a sexist attitude! Aren't there women in your precious Underground?"

"A few, but they are of a different ilk." He leaned down to kiss her neck. "Why are we arguing when we could be making love? I got this hotel room so we could be alone tonight. Let's go to bed."

She wiggled from his embrace. "Oh, no, you don't. You're not going to distract me again while we're having a serious discussion. As to my training, when my brothers get back from their sojourn, they will help me train." She folded her arms over her satin-clad breasts. She looked so sexy in her emerald-green teddy that he wanted to rip it from her body and fuck her until she was unconscious.

"Did I tell you how beautiful you look tonight? Green is my favorite color." He grinned at her.

"Stop trying to change the subject, damn you."

"I thought we were talking about making love, because I sure want to make love to you now. My dick is hard and you need be sitting on it." He licked his lips suggestively.

"You are being a big fat unreasonable jackass, and no amount of seduction will change my mind on this matter." Sasha presented her back to him.

He knew he had pissed her off, but he couldn't help it. He didn't wish to discuss her joining him and his brothers, and his horniness was getting the better of him. He was eager to get between her legs.

Niccolo slowly walked up behind her and pulled her against his chest. Her back was rigid and she didn't respond to his touch. He kissed the delectable curve of her shoulder. "Come on, sweetheart, don't be mad. We'll discuss it later, all right? Besides, I know you want me, too. I can smell your hot little pussy. I bet it's getting wet as you think about my cock sliding into you. Your cunt will be so creamy for me as I move in and out. I won't stop even if you beg me to because I want you to cum for me, over and over again. I want to hear you scream my name as you climax for me, and let all that sweet cream run down your thighs so I can lick it up." Niccolo smiled. "Would you like me to fasten my mouth over your pussy and run my tongue over your clit?"

It seemed his words of seduction were working. Sasha shivered and relaxed against him.

"Niccolo, you're not going to change my mind."

"I know, sweetheart, but we'll talk later, okay?" He ran his tongue along the side of her neck before lifting the heavy curtain of her sable hair. Niccolo pressed kisses against the nape of her neck. "You taste delicious. Would you deny me?"

"You know I won't, you big jerk."

He turned her around to face him. There was a vulnerable gleam in her eyes and he wanted to wipe all her worries away. His emotions for her were so deep at the moment that he wasn't even sure there were words to express how he felt. But he could show her.

He supposed he loved her, but it felt much deeper than the mundane love poets spouted off, or the silly, soap opera type of love. Instead, this feeling burned him to his very soul, making him ache for her when she was near, dream about her while he slept, and jealous of anyone else she bestowed her attention on. His love was dark, hungry, erotic, and intense to the point that he cursed himself for even doubting this woman was his bloodmate.

The love he'd had for Petra, induced by Ivan's spell, couldn't approach these feelings for Sasha. Right now, she looked so beautiful, her dark eyes staring at him with so much trust and desire. His head dipped to taste the sweetness of her slightly parted lips. Each time they kissed was a marvel, no matter how many times their lips met.

*Dio*, she was sweet.

He felt her tongue dart out to meet his, and then shyly retreat. He cupped her face to deepen the kiss and he felt her tongue come out again. This time it was much bolder, tasting and exploring his mouth. He liked it. It filled his body with a pounding lust to know Sasha wanted him as much as he wanted her.

She pulled back slightly to trace the outline of his lips with her tongue. She gave him a little smile. "I love the way you taste."

"I love the way you taste me."

"How about getting out of those clothes so I can get a better look at that beautiful body of yours?" She walked over to the bed. The thin spaghetti straps on her teddy slid down her shoulders. She pushed one off to reveal one rose-tipped breast. Niccolo's mouth went dry as she stuck her finger into her mouth and slowly pulled it out to circle the taut peak that crowned her small but perfectly shaped breast.

"Do you like this?"

"Hell, yeah," he answered, stripping his clothes off in a hurry. He had to have her and if he didn't get some pussy now, he thought he'd go crazy.

"Oh, no, you don't." She shook her head and held up her hand as he moved toward her. He halted.

"What?" he demanded impatiently.

"I don't want you to touch me until I say so."

"You're being ridiculous, woman. Give me some pussy." He took another step forward and ran into an invisible barrier. If he had to deal with one more damn barrier, he swore to God someone would get the fucking of their life...and that someone was going to be Sasha. He would fuck her so hard and long that not only would she not be able to walk straight, but her pussy and ass would be sore from how much he would use her hot little body.

"Remove this barrier, Sasha."

"Why should I? You are denying me something I want, so it's only fair that I do the same."

"What the hell are you talking about?"

"I want to help in your missions."

"No, Sasha."

"Okay. I guess you'll have to suffer." She got to her knees in the middle of the bed and slowly slid her teddy down her body, revealing both of her breasts. He was dying to wrap his mouth around them. Sasha cupped her breasts in her hands, squeezing them. She moaned deep in her throat.

"It's really too bad these aren't your hands touching me. I bet you can smell my pussy from where you're standing. I bet you can tell how wet I am."

He threw his fist out, but the barrier did not budge. "Dammit, Sasha, how are you holding that barrier up without your hands?" he asked.

She shrugged. "With my mind, I guess."

It dawned on him that perhaps Sasha was indeed a very powerful witch. Maybe there was something to that birthmark after all. Nevertheless, it didn't matter how powerful she was, he wasn't going to let her join the Underground.

Maybe if he told her what she wanted to hear she would give him what he wanted. "Okay, okay. You win. Whatever you want is yours," he said gruffly.

She paused as though considering his words. Then she gave him a lazy smile. "Lip service is not enough. I don't believe you're sincere."

Niccolo grabbed his cock, which was so hard by now that he could barely think straight. "Look at me! Can't you see I'm suffering?"

"Mmm, your cock does look like it needs some pussy."

"You're damn right it does, and if you don't give me some now, I won't be held responsible for what will happen next."

She laughed at him as she leaned back to discard her teddy. She tossed it in his direction.

"*Strega*, you will pay for this," he said with narrowed eyes.

"We'll see," she sing-songed. Sasha lay back on the bed and spread her legs wide to reveal the delicious pinkness of her cunt. Niccolo grabbed his cock in his fist, stroking himself as he watched her dip two fingers inside of her wet little hole.

"Oh, yeah," she moaned

How could she do this to him? In his long lifetime, he had been tortured, beaten up, and even been set on fire once, but nothing compared with the excruciating pain he was experiencing at this moment.

He watched in tortured fascination as she fucked herself with her fingers. He wanted very badly to be those fingers. "Come on, Sasha. Have mercy on me," he begged.

She ignored him, moaning in response. Her body writhed and wiggled on the covers. He could tell she was enjoying this act of exhibitionism. His mouth went dry and his balls began to throb. She removed the damp fingers from her cunt and slid them along her body in an upward motion until they reached her mouth.

Sasha slid her cream-dampened fingers between her lips. Niccolo could feel the adrenaline pumping through his veins. It should have been his mouth tasting the sweet juice of her pussy.

He had had enough. With every ounce of his strength he slammed into the barrier, shattering it. Sasha sat up with a startled look on her face. "That's right, *strega*, you thought you could deny me, but you will learn otherwise."

She scooted back on the bed, but he grabbed her by the ankle and pulled her back toward him. Niccolo fell on top of her and, without the slightest hesitation, parted her legs and thrust into her with such force she screamed with joy.

He gripped her thighs and began to plow into her like a man possessed. "This will teach you to deny me," he said roughly, reveling in the tightness of her pussy around his cock. She was so wet for him that her pussy dripped with the evidence of her desire each time his cock pounded into her.

"Oh, yeah, sweetheart. You like this, don't you?"

She shook her head back and forth. "Oh, God, yes! Fuck me, fuck me, fuck me!" she screamed, thrusting her hips upwards.

"You little tease. You enjoy this, don't you?"

Her smile was answer enough.

"You know what I want to hear, don't you, Sasha?"

"This is your pussy! Yours." She groaned in acquiescence.

"You're damn right it is, and don't you forget it either."

He fucked her like a madman, keeping up a frenzied pace that would probably have killed a non-immortal woman, but

Sasha took the forceful entrance of his cock as if she couldn't get enough. When her pussy muscles finally tightened around his dick and she screamed her release, he continued to fuck her.

He was a man of his word and he fully intended to exact full payment by the end of the night.

## Chapter Nineteen

Sasha was indeed sore when she woke up the next morning, but absolutely nothing could keep the smile off her face. Niccolo had not only screwed her for two hours straight without stopping, making her come several times, but he also had woken her up in the middle of the night and made love to her again with a tenderness that had brought tears to her eyes.

The slow, beautiful, gentle way he had touched her proved his feelings. Though he never uttered the words, she just knew.

His body was still next to hers. She turned around. His eyes were closed; he probably just as exhausted as she was.

Sasha leaned over and placed a soft kiss on his lips. His golden eyes flew open. "Good morning, sleepyhead," she said.

"Good morning, beautiful. I'm pleased to see this wasn't a dream. You're real."

"Of course, I am. Why would you think otherwise?" She stroked his hair-roughened cheek. Her heart swelled with love as she absorbed every intricate detail of his features, from the sensual curve of his lips to the shape of his brow.

"I feared that when I woke up you would be gone. For a long time I've known that it was you in my heart, but because of that damn spell and my own stupidity, I could not admit my true feelings. Every time I dreamed about you, I would wake up alone. Now you're here with me, I can hardly believe it. I love you, Sasha."

She gasped in delight. He'd made her wildest dream come true! He'd said he loved her, too. For so long she had longed for this moment and wondered what she would say in response, but now that the time was here, she was at a loss for words.

He looked at her with an expectant gleam in his eye. "Well?"

"I love you, too, Niccolo, but you already know that."

"Yes, but I need to hear you say the words. I get scared, too, you know."

"Really? I didn't know you were scared of anything," she said in awe. Was this her fearless Niccolo? He'd always hidden his vulnerable side from her. It only made her love him more that he could open up to her this way now. She felt a tear escape from the corner of her eye. He brushed the wetness away and pulled her closer to him.

His body felt warm, welcoming, and solid. She knew this was where she belonged, and she never wanted to leave the protection of his arms.

"Of course I get scared of things. I feared for Jagger's safety. I feared I would never be the same after my run-in with your family. I feared you would stop loving me. And now I fear losing you."

"I will never stop loving you. I don't think I'm capable of loving anyone else. Though I've only ever been with you, I saw how my sister went through men with no love or feeling. It was repugnant. I waited for the right man to come into my life, and I'm glad I did."

"I'm glad you waited, too, because I can't take the thought of you with other men."

"Who would have thought you'd be the jealous type?" She smiled at him.

"Haven't you figured it out? We vampires are a very possessive lot, especially when it comes to our women. You should have seen my brother Marco with his bloodmate. He drove the poor woman absolutely nuts, and she started out as a human, so you can imagine what she must have gone through."

"Poor thing. She'd have to have balls of steel to deal with one of the Grimaldis."

"She's very brave. I think you two will get on well."

"I would love to meet her. It's nice of her and your brother to let Jagger stay with them for a little while."

"I'm sure Romeo is keeping him entertained."

She groaned. "Our son will be thoroughly corrupted."

Niccolo chuckled.

"Don't laugh. Can you imagine what kind of trouble he would get into after hanging out with Romeo for a while?"

"I'm sure he'll be okay. As you pointed out earlier, he's a man and it's up to him to make his own decisions."

She pouted. "Do you have to throw my words back in my face?"

"Of course." He winked at her. "I love the way you say 'our son' so naturally. I feel a little cheated that I missed so much of his life."

"Do you want more children?"

He hesitated for a moment, and she feared he would say no. Instead, he took her face into his hands and kissed her deeply. "I would love to have another child with you. We make beautiful children together, don't you think?"

"Yes, we do, so why am I'm sensing a 'but'?"

"Thirty years have been wasted. Thirty years the two of us could have been together. I want you all to myself for a while and I'd like to become closer to the son I already have."

"That sounds fair."

"I think so. One day we will have more children, but not right now. Agreed?"

"Agreed." She smiled at him; her heart felt like it would overflow with all the love she felt for him.

"What are you thinking about?"

"I'm thinking about how much I love you. It's still hard for me to believe we're here together like this."

"I know." He kissed her again, cuddling her in his arms. He must have held her for several minutes, before he made a move to get up. "We should probably get dressed. Everyone will be at Marco's house soon to discuss what's going to happen next."

"I was serious about being by your side and seeing this thing through."

"And I've already told you no."

"Let's not go down that path again. I won't change my mind about this."

"Nor will I. Don't you know what it would do to me if something happened to you?"

"Yes, because it's the same way I'd feel if something happened to you. Look, I'm no longer helpless and my powers will grow stronger each day. I can feel it. You heard my father, there are more than rogue vampires involved: shifters, witches, and warlocks have joined forces. You'll need my skills. I'll contact my brothers and perhaps they will help us."

Niccolo didn't look like he would reply, but he finally did with a sigh. "We'll see," was all he said.

Sasha decided not to push the subject any further, knowing that she could wear him down a little later. At least "we'll see" was not "no". "Okay." She kissed his cheek while her hand slid down his chest to travel further until she reached his cock.

"You're ready again?" she teased. "Are you in the perpetual state of horniness?"

"For you, yes."

"Do we have time for a fuck, before we go?"

"Of course, we do. If not, we'll make time."

He pulled her against him. "I owe you something first."

"What?" she asked.

"A spanking."

<><><><><>

"Honey, are you sure you have to leave so soon? You only got here yesterday. I thought you were going to stay for the week." Maggie looked at her daughter, who was standing at the door with her travel pack. She seemed distressed.

"Yeah, I'm sorry, but something came up. Besides, I told Daddy I'd visit him before I went back down south."

215

Jagger watched mother and daughter, wishing he'd had more time with Camryn. Perhaps he had come on a little too strong, but if there was something he had learned about being a vampire, it was that they went for what they wanted, and he couldn't remember wanting anyone like he did Camryn Williams. She made him feel like a teenager again.

He didn't know if he wanted her just for sex or for something more, but in the short time they'd spent under the same roof to together, he determined that no matter how much she ran, he'd catch her.

Jagger had tried getting to know her better but was thwarted by her at every attempt he had made. He realized he should probably save himself the aggravation and leave her alone, but all during dinner the prior night, he hadn't been able to look away from her. When she spoke to her mother or his Uncle GianMarco, she would smile, showing off the deepest dimples he'd ever seen. But when she turned those big brown eyes on him, she seemed to be looking right through him as though he weren't there. It was frustrating.

She'd soon learn it wouldn't be easy getting rid of him.

His Uncle GianMarco walked over to give her a hug. "Take care of yourself, brat. We wish you could have stayed a little longer, but at least you won't have anything to complain about when you go to sleep tonight."

Camryn giggled. "Yeah, I'm looking forward to a decent night's sleep. The two of you hump like bunnies and you're loud about it."

Maggie looked scandalized. "Camryn!"

"Mom, come on, if the two of you weren't always carrying on, I wouldn't have any ammunition." Camryn checked her watch. "Okay, I'm going to hit the road to beat the rush-hour traffic." Maggie gave her daughter a hug, tears glistening in her eyes.

"Do I not merit a hug?" Jagger asked, stepping forward.

Camryn held out her hand with obvious reluctance. She ought to have known better. Jagger grabbed her hand and pulled her against him. He closed his arms tightly around her and leaned down to whisper in her ear, "This isn't over." Then he released her.

Camryn's pursed her lips and glared at him. "Goodbye," she said with finality, turning away to face her mother. "Do you want to walk me to my car?"

Maggie grinned and took her hand. "Of course!"

"Marc, tell Romeo I said goodbye, and to stay out of trouble." Camryn smiled at her stepfather.

"Ha! As if he would listen. At this very moment, he's probably in a bar fight." GianMarco chuckled.

Jagger made a move to follow them, but his uncle gripped his arm, holding him back. "Leave them be. They need their moment together. My wife doesn't get to see her children as often as she likes."

Jagger stepped back reluctantly as he watched Camryn and Maggie's retreating figures. What was it about that particular woman that made him act this way? He had been with women more beautiful and sophisticated than her, yet she was the one who sparked a fire in his blood.

"She's a lovely girl, isn't she?"

Jagger looked over at his uncle, whose eyes had not left his wife's retreating form.

"What are you talking about?" Jagger feigned a nonchalance he didn't feel.

"Your mind is open to me, but I don't have to read your thoughts to know of your interest in my stepdaughter. You couldn't keep your eyes off her at dinner last night, and I suspect her early departure may be the result of something that happened between the two of you yesterday."

Jagger realized there was no point in denying it. "I'm sorry. I didn't mean to run her off."

"Perhaps not, but you have to be careful when revealing yourself to mortals. I've lived among them most of my life and have revealed myself to only a very few. They can be skittish, and sometimes don't know how to react to things they don't understand. It's human nature, unfortunately."

"Yes, I realize this. I've lived among mortals myself, but Maggie seems to have embraced our lifestyle."

"Yes, she's adjusted to our ways now, but she was frightened in the beginning, and there was a difficult transition period. It wasn't an instantaneous acceptance. One thing you will learn about Camryn, if you haven't already, is that she's a very single-minded young lady. I'm not saying that's good or bad, but she's young, only twenty-two, and generally mortals her age see things in black and white. In the beginning she was very uneasy around me, and even now, I feel she isn't quite as accepting as she appears to be. Don't get me wrong, I know she's happy for her mother, but there's still the element of fear."

"How can she fear us when she won't give us a chance?"

"She is giving us a chance, in her way. She just needs time."

"That's what you say, but according to the stories I've heard, you took what you wanted. Why can't I?"

"Well, my circumstances were a little different. Look, it's obvious to me you're going to do what you want to, but I will caution you to take it easy. Give her some time."

"How much time?"

"As much as she needs. You'll need to exert a little patience. I know you're frustrated and you think you want her—"

"I know I want her."

"Okay, you know you want her, but does she want you?"

Jagger paused. It didn't seem like she did, but he knew if she would just give him a chance she would. "Maybe not now, but eventually she will. She has to. Why else do I feel this instant pull toward her?"

GianMarco looked as though he wanted to say something but changed his mind. Jagger wished his mind-reading abilities were more adept so that he could tell what the older vampire was thinking.

"Tell me what I need to do to win her."

GianMarco stared at him long and hard before he answered. "I hope you can appreciate my dilemma here. You're my nephew and I care about you, but my first loyalty is with my wife and immediate family. Were Camryn any other woman, I would tell you to take her, but she's not. She's my stepdaughter, therefore under my protection, and I will not see her hurt."

"I would never hurt her."

"I know you don't intend to, but if you force your attention on her, it will only make her run further away, and that would upset her mother. As you can tell, she's already upset because her daughter is leaving earlier than planned. The last thing Maggie needs is to be upset in her condition."

"I understand you, Uncle, but just so we understand each other...if time is what she needs, I will give it to her, but I won't wait forever."

GianMarco looked at him with a faint smile. "Perhaps you're exactly what Camryn needs, but be warned, she's quite a handful. I wish you luck. You're going to need it."

## Epilogue

Everyone in the room wore grim expressions as Dante went over what he expected each of them to do. Niccolo could feel the tension inside Sasha and wished he could comfort her.

"Marco, although we need as many bodies as we can get for what's about to go down, more than ever, you will need to keep your wife safe. I can't and don't expect you to leave her in her condition. Don't let her out of the house unless she's with you or a member of the Underground."

Niccolo thought it was odd the way Dante refused to make eye contact with Maggie or, for that matter, even say her name. No one would mention what had happened between them.

"Romeo, I need to talk to you after dinner." Dante then turned to Niccolo. "Nico, I'm going to need you to go to Europe and stick around, because I have a feeling the massacres are not over yet."

"I'm going with him," Sasha added.

"So am I," said Jagger.

"No!" Niccolo shouted to both of them.

"You have to let me help you. You're going to need me," Sasha insisted.

"And I'm not staying behind either when I know you're going to need all the help you can get. I've learned things: secret hideouts, some of the other players involved," Jagger argued.

Niccolo shook his head. "You're too young."

"That is a crock of shit. Was I too young when I killed that rogue? Was I too young when I held off three rogues and two shifters? Papa, I understand you're trying to protect me, but I've been taking care of myself for a long time now. Trust me. I can do this. I understand the danger involved and if I believed for a second that I wasn't up to it, I wouldn't volunteer." Jagger tone said he meant business.

Niccolo opened his mouth to object, but Sasha took his arm and shook her head. "He wants to help. Let him."

"But he's just a kid."

"Maybe to you but he's not. Neither of us needs to be coddled. We're a family now, and Jagger and I want to stay by your side through this thing."

Niccolo knew he was fighting a losing battle as he witnessed their determined looks. "But I'll be devastated if I lose either one of you," he protested.

Jagger walked over and knelt in front of him. "The thought of losing you is not appealing to us either, Papa, but you stick your neck out for the greater good. We know what we're into. We're a team and we'll have each other's backs."

"You're too damned wise for your years, boy." Niccolo muttered.

Sasha's eyes lit up. "We can come with you?"

"Yes, but you will both stay close to me at all times."

"All we want is a chance." She patted his hand with a smug smile before turning back to Dante. Niccolo had a feeling that he had just been railroaded. No matter, he would exact his payment later tonight when they were finally alone.

Niccolo squeezed her hand and pulled Jagger close to him. He loved these two more than life itself. Though he knew there were dangerous times ahead, everything would be all right with his woman and his son by his side.

<><><><><><>

Dante leaned against the side of the house. Everyone else was inside enjoying one of Maggie's peach cobblers. It was getting difficult to act naturally around her as though nothing had happened. He glanced at his watch. He had told Romeo to meet him outside five minutes ago. Where the hell was he?

Just as Dante turned to go back into the house, Romeo showed up. "What the hell took you so long?"

"Maggie insisted I finish dessert first, not that I needed much arm twisting. The woman is a genius in the kitchen."

"I didn't ask you outside to talk about her cooking."

"What's up with you tonight? You barely said two words to Maggie. I thought you liked her."

"Let's drop the subject," Dante spoke between clenched teeth.

Romeo shrugged, with a nonplussed expression on his face. "So, did you want to discuss with me in private?"

"A war is about to happen if drastic measures aren't taken."

"What do you need?"

"I want you to take care of the heads of Council."

"What exactly do you want me to do?"

"Kill them. Every single one of them."

## About the Author

New York Times and USA Today Bestselling Author Eve has always enjoyed creating characters and stories from an early age. As a child she was always getting into mischief, so when she lost her television privileges (which was often), writing was her outlet. Her stories have gotten quite a bit spicier since then! When she's not writing or spending time with her family, Eve is reading, baking, traveling or kicking butt in 80's trivia. She loves hearing from her readers. She can be contacted through her website at: www.evevaughn.com.

More Books From Eve Vaughn:


Finding Divine

Whatever He Wants

The Kyriakis Curse:
Book One of the Kyriakis Series

The Kyriakis Legacy:
Book Two of the Kyriakis Series

GianMarco:
Book One of the Blood Brothers Series

Niccolo:
Book Two of the Blood Brothers Series

Romeo:
Book Three of the Blood Brothers Series

Jagger:
Book Four of the Blood Brothers Series

Dante:
Book Five of the Blood Brothers Series

Made in the USA
Monee, IL
07 November 2021